P9-AQS-616

2023

WITHDRAWN

AND ME

Meira Drazin

SCHOLASTIC PRESS ✳ NEW YORK

Text copyright © 2022 by Meira Drazin

Jacket illustrations copyright © 2022 by Shamar Knight-Justice

All rights reserved. Published by Scholastic Press, an imprint of Scholastic Inc., *Publishers since 1920*. SCHOLASTIC, SCHOLASTIC PRESS, and associated logos are trademarks and/or registered trademarks of Scholastic Inc.

The publisher does not have any control over and does not assume any responsibility for author or third-party websites or their content.

No part of this publication may be reproduced, stored in a retrieval system, or transmitted in any form or by any means, electronic, mechanical, photocopying, recording, or otherwise, without written permission of the publisher. For information regarding permission, write to Scholastic Inc., Attention: Permissions Department, 557 Broadway, New York, NY 10012.

This book is a work of fiction. Names, characters, places, and incidents are either the product of the author's imagination or are used fictitiously, and any resemblance to actual persons, living or dead, business establishments, events, or locales is entirely coincidental.

Library of Congress Cataloging-in-Publication Data available

ISBN 978-1-338-15543-3

1 2022

Printed in the U.S.A.   23

First edition, October 2022

To Hillel,
and to Niva, Shai, Izzy, and Emmanuelle
—my own "big family"—
with love

Shabbat

CHAPTER 1

OUR SHUL

"Are you going to ask him for the Yum-Yums?" I whisper to Honey. It's Saturday morning and we are scampering across the lobby of our synagogue on our way to the candyman. Mr. Eisner only gives Yum-Yums, the best kind of lollypop, to the kids he really likes.

"Don't we deserve the best?" Honey says with a wink as we reach the door to the men's section.

"You two think you're so special, don't you?" someone calls to us. We turn around. Honey's younger sister Miriam is sitting on the counter of the cloak-room, watching us as she sucks on a lollypop—the bad kind. Miriam is ten and very annoying.

"I don't think it, I *know* it," Honey calls back, putting her arm around me and sticking her tongue out at Miriam. I don't feel special like Honey is, but I grin anyway and put my arm around my best friend. Then we each use our other hand to pull open the double doors to the main sanctuary.

As the doors close softly behind us, I inhale the

familiar smell of woolen prayer shawls, dark suits, leathery aftershave, and old prayer books. Everyone in front of us is standing and swaying slightly, many with their prayer shawls draped over their heads. Honey catches my eye and I nod: We'll wait back here by the door until the silent Amidah prayer is over.

"Hi, Milla!" My little brother, Max, whisper-shouts, spying me from my dad's regular spot about a third of the way into the sanctuary. Max waves and scoots over on the velvet-cushioned bench of the synagogue pew to make room for me.

"Shhhh." A few men cloaked in their cream and black-striped prayer shawls turn around. My face heats. Do they stare at me an extra beat before turning their backs again? My father looks up from his siddur for a moment to give me a smile before looking down at the prayer book and continuing the silent meditation. I give a small wave back at Max, pointing to Mr. Eisner to indicate that I'm just making a quick candy run.

When I was Max's age I also used to come to shul early every Shabbat morning with my dad. I'd sit with him here in the main sanctuary, quietly watching all the men praying, my eyes inevitably drawn to where

Honey's dad always sits. She and her siblings were usually squished two or three to a seat, jostling one another and loudly saying "shush"—until eventually Mr. Wine would release them to attend the children's services. More likely they would run to the cloakroom, or the lower level where the kitchens are, or the stairs to the ladies' section, or any of the other spots the kids in our synagogue like to hang out. That's when I would whisper to my dad that I was going with Honey and before he'd even finished nodding his assent, I was down the aisle.

"C'mon." Honey tugs my arm now as the prayer ends and people sit. "Good Shabbos, Mr. Eisner," she says as soon as we get to his seat, wishing him a good Sabbath and offering her hand for a handshake.

"Good Shabbos, ladies," Mr. Eisner says, shaking Honey's hand and then mine. "So good to see you both again." Honey and I have been away at sleepaway camp together for the last seven weeks.

"Next year we'll send you a postcard," Honey says with a grin.

"Marvelous!" Mr. Eisner says, his eyes twinkling. "Perhaps I shall send one back."

"Even better, you can send us some candy,"

Honey says, and I cover my mouth with my hand. I don't know how she can be so bold, so chutzpadik—and with a grown-up!

But Mr. Eisner claps his hands together now as he beams. "Always negotiating, this one," he says. "You strike a tough bargain, young lady. But it's a deal."

Honey laughs and offers her hand again for Mr. Eisner to shake and seal the deal, which he does. He puts out his hand to me and I give him a firm handshake too.

"So—" Honey says. "Any Yum-Yums today?"

"Please," I add.

"For you two, of course," Mr. Eisner responds with another beam. "You know I save them for my favorite kids."

"Thanks!" we both whisper with gusto as he hands us the lollypops. Then Honey tugs my arm again and we run back down the aisle and out of the sanctuary.

"Oh, hi, Miriam," Honey says, smoothly opening the wrapper of her lollypop as we pass by the cloakroom. Miriam's still on the counter, watching a group of girls her age playing a hand-clapping game underneath the coatracks.

"Well, you won't be getting those for long!"

Miriam calls after us. "Soon you're going to be sitting next to Aginéni and hoping she doesn't offer you some cod liver oil." Miriam laughs.

Aginéni is an old lady who sits in the front row of the balcony women's section every Shabbat and festival, in a seat she staked for herself before our parents were even born.

"At least I'm not afraid of her," Honey calls back. "Like *someone* I know."

On cue, we both cough into our fists and say, "Miriam." Of course, I'm totally scared of Aginéni too—everyone is, except maybe for Honey—but we both crack up as we turn away again.

When we reach the stairs that lead to the lower level, I say, "It's true though about Mr. Eisner. I mean, your bat mitzvah is in March." I don't add that mine is in June. We both know that once Honey is twelve and too old for the men's section, there's no way I will go to Mr. Eisner by myself.

"So we have until March," Honey says, hopping onto the banister and sliding down sidesaddle.

"I can't believe we're starting middle school," I say, meeting her at the bottom of the stairs. "My mom told me all the sixth-grade girls do a bat mitzvah presentation at the end of the year. Does your school do something too?"

Honey is still sitting on the bottom curl of the banister swinging her legs, but a weird expression has crossed her face. "Huh?"

"Does your school have a bat mitzvah presentation or something?" I repeat. Honey and I don't go to the same school.

"Oh, um, maybe," she says.

I raise my eyebrows. My nine years of experience being best friends with Honey Wine tells me this is something she would know.

"What's wrong?" I say.

"Nothing," she says. Then the uncomfortable expression leaves her face and is replaced by her familiar grin. "C'mon, let's go see if we can sneak into the kitchen and get some kiddush food." She hops down from the banister and loops her arm through mine.

My mouth waters at the thought of hot potato kugel, maybe with a side of salty herring on a cracker. I grin back and give her arm a squeeze.

Everything is always better with Honey by my side.

CHAPTER 2

HONEY'S HOUSE

The next Friday night, I wriggle out of the cardigan my mother insisted I take and bounce down my driveway to my favorite place in the world: Honey's house. It's Labor Day weekend, and the twilight is warm, the sky a deep blue above me as I take the narrow dirt shortcut and emerge onto Honey's crescent-shaped street. At the deepest part of the curve, the Wines' red-bricked house sits on a wide double lot like its arms are outstretched in welcome.

I bound up the front steps. The big brass knocker that used to be attached to their heavy front door has fallen off. We don't use the doorbell on Shabbat, so I knock as hard as I can with my bare knuckles. This is mostly for show. In the spot where other people have a lock, the Wines have a little gold keypad fitted to the door, and like any neighborhood kid worth their salt, I know that to get into the Wines' you just press 61318, then turn the dial and push the door open.

"Helloooo?!" I call, opening the door for myself. "Good Shabbos!" I hear the light sound of women's voices coming from deeper in the house. The men must not be back from shul yet. I drop my cardigan on the front-staircase banister, right on top of the spare wig Mrs. Wine plunks on her head whenever she leaves the house, and follow the sound down a wide hallway to a broadly lit scene in the living room.

Mrs. Wine is ushering a woman with a shaved head and nose ring to an armchair, listening intently to what she is saying and nodding. Shabbat at the Wines' always feature an array of guests, from Mr. Wine's students, to single cousins, to dignitaries in the Jewish community, family friends and friends of the Wine kids, and even random people who don't have anywhere else to go. A case in point is Susie, who Mrs. Wine settles herself next to on the love seat: Susie is always here, but even after all this time of being friends with Honey, I actually have no idea if she is a long-term hanger-on or some kind of relative.

Miriam gets up from the wingback chair and squeezes herself onto Mrs. Wine's other side. Honey is sitting cross-legged on the rug, fixing two little blond ponytails on her sister Dan-Dan's head. Then she turns Dan-Dan to face her, cocking her head to one side to evaluate her handiwork. They haven't noticed me yet, so I turn to one of the glass-doored cabinets that flank the archway to take a peek at the figurines inside: My favorite is an old lady holding balloons. My fingers itch to play with it.

"Milla!" Honey says, spying me and getting up. "I have big news! You're not going to believe it!"

"Oh yeah," Miriam calls to me. "She wants to tell you—"

"Don't you dare, Miriam," Honey cuts her short with an imperious glare. "Ima said we could each tell our friends."

"And this is Honey, my oldest daughter," Mrs. Wine says to the guest I don't recognize, gesturing in our direction while giving a stern look to Miriam.

Honey raises her hand slightly by way of greeting. "I might be the oldest girl, but I am also the *middle* child of seven kids. Just in case you thought *you* had issues." She folds her arms and waits for the woman to look impressed.

"Wow," the woman says. "Intense."

"My oldest daughter and a blessing," Mrs. Wine says, smiling now.

"What does that make me?" Miriam asks. "A curse?"

Honey and I exchange smirks. "You said it, not me," Honey tells her. I bite my lip to keep from laughing.

"Miriam, of course you are a blessing too. Baruch Hashem, you are all brachas," Mrs. Wine says firmly, thanking God for these blessings.

"And I'm Dan-Dan, the littlest blessing," adds Dan-Dan, smiling sweetly.

"Her real name is Daniella," Miriam informs the lady. "One day she's going to hate having such a baby name and all I will say is, I TOLD YOU SO."

Dan-Dan gives Miriam an impressive side-eye for a four-year-old and goes to sit in Mrs. Wine's lap. Honey tugs my sleeve and starts pulling me out of the living room.

"And this is Milla Bloom, my Honey's best friend," Mrs. Wine says, gesturing in my direction. I blush and wave shyly, basking in the glow of Mrs. Wine's warmth and my title.

"Like a sister," Honey says, putting her arm around me.

Miriam scowls.

Honey tugs my arm again, and I let her pull me out the door and across the hall to the dining room.

She shuts the French doors and then leans against them. "Milla," she says, her eyes sparkling.

"What?" I say excitedly.

"Hang on," Honey says. She whirls around, lifting the tablecloth and its plastic covering. Honey's younger brother, Aaron, six and blond-haired like Honey and Dan-Dan, is sitting cross-legged under the table, ripping playing cards in half one by one.

"Hi, Aaron," I say.

"Hi, Aaron," he says, which is his way of saying hi back to me. Then he screeches and throws two halves of a king of hearts in front of him.

Honey lifts a finger to tell me "one minute" and disappears under the table.

I look around at the dining room: A nine-branched candelabra sits stately on the sideboard, burning bright with the Shabbat candles. Over a shiny plastic tablecloth, the table glitters with delicate white dishes, with tiny midnight-blue-and-gold flowers around the edges, that the Wines only use on Shabbat and festivals. My mother looks like she's smelled old milk whenever she sees plastic in someone's dining room. But if Mrs. Wine didn't have it, she would probably have to buy a new tablecloth every week. At the

Wines', somebody is always spilling something.

Glancing at the wallpaper above the sideboard, I can see it is peeling at the edges, and I smile fondly at the grandfather clock in the corner, which has read a quarter to three since as long as I've known how to tell time. I do think that the Wines are very on top of their home though, which is different than their house. There aren't many rules at the Wines', but the ones they do have—like no gossiping—pretty much never get broken. And as always, at the foot of the table, on Mrs. Wine's sparkling china plate, there are seven white folded pieces of paper. I let my eyes linger on them while listening to Honey's soothing tones coming from under the table.

After another minute, she lifts up the tablecloth and crawls out. I see Aaron now calmly making piles out of the card halves.

"Okay, so—" Honey says to me.

"Good Shabbos! Good Shabbos!" Mr. Wine and Honey's older brothers call from the front door.

"Ugh!" Honey groans, flopping down from her knees onto the thick carpet.

"Just tell me!" I say. "Quickly, before they come in here."

"No, I want to do it privately—" she says.

"I. SEE. DEAD. PEOPLE," Josh says, throwing open the French doors to the dining room. He stalks toward me, his arms out like a zombie. Josh is the oldest of the Wines, mischievous and popular. He shaves, has his driver's license, and goes to the big kosher deli with friends on Saturday nights. He likes to make fun of me for my look of shock when I found out Mrs. Wine is a chevra kadisha volunteer. She helps prepare dead bodies for burial.

"Very funny," I tell him sarcastically, even as I flush with pleasure. I love the inside joke.

The dining room begins filling with people. "Good Shabbos, Ima," Ezra says, bending down to give Mrs. Wine a hug. Ezra is next in line after Josh, bigger and quieter. He's going into eleventh grade.

"This one looks like a brute, but he's the biggest softie you'll ever meet," Mrs. Wine says, giving him a squeeze.

"Ima," he says, reddening.

Introductions are made with all the guests, including two stragglers Mr. Wine has picked up at shul. Mrs. Wine bustles around adding place settings while Mr. Wine begins singing "Shalom Aleichem" to welcome the day of rest. Everyone joins in singing as Mrs. Wine points to where each of us should sit. I stick close to Honey and pray I get a Wine kid and not a stranger on my other side. While Honey would be equally comfortable making conversation with a celebrity or a lamppost, let's just say that I am not able to do that.

As if on cue, the woman from the living room starts loudly humming a completely different song and swaying. I bite my lip, but no one else bats an eye.

Josh punches Ezra in the arm, hard. "Sucker punch, sucker," Josh says.

"Raise you one, sucker," Ezra says, gleefully pummeling him back.

"Abba, it's *my* turn to sit next to you," Miriam complains to Mr. Wine, who is enthusiastically singing off-key while trying to wipe up the deep red wine he has accidentally glugged over the side of his silver kiddush cup. It is running a small river over the edge of the plastic tablecloth and down toward the carpet.

"Want to hear the best joke ever?" Micah says to me, his copper hair newly cropped since camp and some freckles standing out against his summer tan. He's next in age after Ezra and is starting ninth grade, but it always seems to me that he has to work hard to keep up with his older brothers.

"Sure, why not," I say, trying to sound casual. Of course, I'd rather *die* than let Honey know I think Micah is cute.

"Two elephants are sitting in a bath and one elephant says to the other, 'Pass me the soap.' And the other elephant says: 'No soap radio!'" Micah laughs. "Get it?" He gives me a toothy smile.

I roll my eyes and laugh. "You want me to pretend I get it, even though it makes no sense, so you can laugh at me."

"Not funny," Honey informs Micah.

"Yom hashishi!" Mr. Wine says, giving up on his soggy pile of napkins and beginning the blessing over the wine.

"Abba," Miriam interrupts, standing right in front of him. "You forgot to give us our brachas."

"Ah," Mr. Wine says. "Miriameleh, what would I do without you?" Miriam glances at Honey with a smirk before bowing her head so that Mr. Wine can place his hands on it and whisper the traditional blessing over the children.

"Let God bless you and watch over you," he begins

in Hebrew. I stand in my spot while the Wine kids line up in front of Mr. Wine for their turn.

"Get out of my seat," Honey says to Micah when she gets back, stomping on his foot. "Milla's *my* guest."

Micah smiles winningly at a skinny man with wispy hair until the man moves down one chair toward Ezra; Micah slides into the seat on my other side. "I'm funny, right?" Micah says to me, wagging his eyebrows up and down.

"Nope," I say, giggling.

Mr. Wine holds the large silver kiddush goblet up high and loudly begins the blessing over the wine again, the room quieting down. When it is over and everyone is drinking wine or grape juice in thimble-sized silver cups, Mrs. Wine hands a piece of white folded paper to each of her kids.

"Good Shabbos, my loved ones."

"Good Shabbos, Ima," they chorus.

Then there is quiet rustling as the Wine children read their notes. Ezra, who is captain of every sports team and apparently feared even by the kids on the non-Jewish hockey teams, brushes a tear off his cheek and gulps his grape juice. Josh glances at his quickly before going over to read Aaron's to him. Honey smiles as she reads her note, then turns to read Dan-Dan's to her, accidentally sweeping her own note onto the floor. I pick it up and take a quick peek before putting it on her plate.

Dear Honey-loo, it says in Mrs. Wine's quick scrawl, *I was so proud of you for watching Aaron and Dan-Dan yesterday when I got my phone call from the chevra kadisha. You are a model older sister, and I know you will rise to your new circumstances and embrace any challenges. I love you. Ima.*

New circumstances? Is this bat mitzvah related? I think about Honey's expression in shul last week and suddenly wonder if it is connected to her big news.

Mr. Wine claps his hands to get everyone's attention. "May I invite you all to netilat yadayim, our ritual cleansing of the hands before we bless the challah. And let me remind you"—he holds up one finger in a fake serious way—"that between the blessing over our hands and the Hamotzi blessing over the challah, we do not talk until we have taken a bite of the bread." He ushers everyone to the kitchen sink.

Even though no one's talking, the Wine kids are snapping towels at each other. Micah flicks water at me, and I dash to hide behind Honey, giggling. Mrs. Wine gives Micah a big "ahem" and puts her hands on his shoulders to march him back to the dining room. Finally, Mr. Wine says, *"Hamotzi lechem min ha'aretz."* He salts the challah, saws the soft braided bread with poppy seeds sprinkled on top into fourteen pieces for everyone sitting at the table tonight, and tosses them into a basket. As the basket makes its way around and each person bites into their piece of challah and is allowed to talk again, the table erupts into laughter and shouting.

"I need Milla's help with the soup!" Honey hollers over the racket, dragging me into the kitchen and then through to the walk-in pantry, firmly shutting the door behind her. The pantry looks like a kosher supermarket and smells like bubble gum and a heady mix of the spices arranged haphazardly in wire baskets.

"Milla!"

"What?" I say.

"I'm coming to your school!" Honey says. "I'm coming to Eden Academy!"

"To visit?"

"No! For good. We got the uniforms today!"

"What?" I say again.

"I wanted to tell you last week in shul, but Ima said we had to wait until we officially got accepted."

I am so shocked, I am speechless.

"Well, say something!" Honey says.

I don't know what else to do, so I start shrieking in excitement. She whoops it up with me. I can't believe that after all this time we are going to go to school together.

"Everything okay?" Mr. Wine calls through the door.

"Yes, Abba!" Honey calls back.

"It's just Milla, Abba," we hear Miriam's muffled voice. "Honey must have told her the big *news*." She says "news" like it smells.

Honey and I make faces at each other. "Wait," I say. "How come you're switching?"

"Well, Aaron's going to Tablet," she says, and I nod in understanding. Aaron is autistic, and Tablet is a program at my school for kids with disabilities. "So we're all switching—me, Miriam, and Dan-Dan."

"I can't believe it. I'm so excited!" I say. It feels

almost too good to be true. I make cheering sounds again, and Honey joins in.

This must be what Mrs. Wine was talking about when she wrote about new circumstances and embracing challenges.

"Don't worry," I tell Honey. "You'll be fine."

"I know," she says. "I'm not worried."

I smile. Of course she isn't. I would be so scared to start a new school. Especially if I'd always gone to an all-girls school and then had to switch to co-ed. Even if it was still an Orthodox school, which mine is, of course. But Honey is Honey. Nothing worries her. I smile again and then sneeze without warning, the spices suddenly tickling my nose.

CHAPTER 3

MY HOUSE

In my house, the furniture is modern and new. The dining room chairs are white leather, and my mother hired an interior designer so that the pillows in the living room match the blinds. The kitchen has stark white counters and stainless steel appliances. Framed artwork hangs at regularly spaced intervals in the front hallway. Our house is not big, but everything in it is deliberate. Even the fake flowers in the downstairs bathroom are always arranged just so.

"Can I go to Honey's house now?" I ask, pushing my seat back from the dining room table. It is Saturday, Shabbat lunch, and we have just finished saying the Grace After Meals—my parents and me saying it silently to ourselves, Max pretending to whisper the words even though he doesn't really know how to read Hebrew (or English) yet. Unless my Aunty Steph is staying with us, my house is so boring on Shabbat afternoons.

"So that's big news, about Honey coming to your class," my mom says, starting to stack the dessert plates and ignoring my question.

"I know!" I say. That's what she said last night when I burst inside after Honey and Ezra walked me home. She didn't look surprised, or anywhere near as thrilled as me. Of course, it turned out that she already knew— she's the chairwoman of the board of my school. (But she never tells me *anything*!) Then, when I woke up this morning, she asked me how I felt about "Honey's big news now that I'd had a chance to sleep on it."

"I'm so excited!" I say again. "Everyone's going to love her."

"I'm sure they will," my mother says, and hands me the white ceramic platter the chocolate rugelech were on. She raises her eyebrows and gestures with her head that I should help clean up by taking it back to the kitchen. I take the last rugeleh and pop it in my mouth, savoring the sweet, doughy pastry.

"Camp for two months, hanging out every Shabbat afternoon, now school together," my dad says mischievously, looking at my mother. "If *I* had to spend all that time with somebody, never mind live with them, I would *definitely* get sick of them."

"Jonathan!" My mother whacks him on the arm. Then she pushes the stack of dirty dessert plates toward him.

"Is that why you travel so much, Daddy?" Max asks. He has a chocolate mustache from the rugelech. "So that you don't get sick of us?"

"What? No—no way, buddy. I would never get sick of you. I was just kidding around." My dad stands up and scoops Max out of the chair next to mine and gives him a hug. "But your mother and Milla on the other hand . . ." He shakes his head sadly.

I laugh even before he waits a beat to wag his eyebrows so Max knows he's still joking. My dad loves to tease us, and he is really good at keeping his face straight while he does it. The trick is to look closely and see if his eyes are smiling.

"Jonathan, be serious for once," my mother says, pushing the stack of dessert plates closer to where he's now standing.

"Of course I'm serious. I'm a serious guy. Who could have more gravitas than a tax lawyer?" My dad winks at me. "You knew that from our very first date."

"I thought your first date was Mom helping you study for an exam," I say, taking the empty dessert platter to the kitchen.

"Which I aced," my dad says, eyes twinkling. My

mother, who was a year above my dad in law school, rolls her eyes to the ceiling.

"Anyway, apparently Judy Wine had a disagreement with Schachter Mesifta's policy over children with disabilities," she says, following me. She's carrying four water glasses in one hand and the pitcher in the other, our dirty napkins crumpled in the crook of her elbow. "And she's pulling all her kids out. Can you imagine, the school her own grandfather founded?"

"Yeah," I say, although I didn't know the part about the disagreement or about Honey's great-grandfather. "It's surprising. But it's good."

"Well, I'm glad Eden Academy partners with Tablet and provides an inclusive Jewish education, and it's great for our school to have the Wines," she says, setting everything down on the counter. She tucks her hair behind her ear, and for a moment, I wonder how she would look wearing a sheitel like Mrs. Wine does. Like a lot of my school friends' mothers, my mom doesn't wear pants, but she only covers her hair—with a hat—when she goes to shul. "How do you really feel about it, Milla? You and Honey have never gone to school together . . ."

"Yes, we did, remember—we *met* at Morah

Nechama's," I say, reminding her how Honey and I became friends. Whenever Morah Nechama sees us in shul, she loves to tell us about how we were always giggling together in a corner, so she encouraged my mother and Mrs. Wine to set up playdates for us.

"That was at a playgroup, when you were two," my mother says.

"We go to camp together," I say.

"Camp is different," my mother points out.

"So going to school together is even better," I say.

"Okay," she says, opening the garbage bin with her foot and dropping the dirty napkins into it.

I put my hand on my waist. "What?" I say.

"Nothing," my mother says.

"Honey coming is good!" I say.

"Okay," she says. "If you say so."

"I *do* say so! Everyone will love her, and she's my best friend."

My mother lets out an exasperated breath. "Fine, but—"

"Lori—" My dad pokes his head into the kitchen and gives my mother a pointed look.

My mother waves her hand to shoo him away and sighs as she turns to me. "It's just—sixth grade was a really big year for me," she says. Then she smiles. "And I'm sure it will be for you too."

I shrug. "Well—" There's a lump starting to form in my throat. "Maybe you could write me and Max notes, like Mrs. Wine does, about why you're proud of us?"

"Milla, you shouldn't need a note to know I'm proud of you. I'm proud of all my children."

"It's just me and Max," I point out.

"Milla Ruth, you're missing the point!" my mother says with a sudden flash of anger that startles me. She only calls me by my full name when she's really upset. She swings the door open hard.

"Sorry!" I say quickly, tears pricking my eyes. My parents spent a lot of time (and money) trying to have more kids. That's why there's such a big age gap between me and Max. And why it's only the two of us.

"It's fine," she says in a pinched voice, motioning for me to come over and holding out her arms so she can give me a hug. The door swings back in and bumps against her, jostling us. "I have two wonderful children who I love very much and who I've given up my career for, with no regrets. *Whatsoever*. And if I had more kids, I wouldn't have as much time to devote to volunteering for your school."

"Group hug!" Max cries, steering my dad toward us. My dad sets the challah board down, crumbs spilling everywhere, and picks up Max, wrapping his other arm around me and my mom.

But then, just as quickly, we are pulling apart. My dad puts Max down and rifles through the newspaper to find the sports section before heading upstairs to bed for a Shabbat afternoon rest. My mother walks back and forth to the kitchen to finish cleaning up; soon she'll find the book review section and also go upstairs to rest. Already the quiet is descending. It's like the heavy velvet cloth covering the bima in synagogue is draping our house, muffling our voices and amplifying other sounds—neighborhood children playing in their backyards, an airplane overhead, the soft hum as the air-conditioning starts up, the clink of my mother loading the dishwasher, the whooshing of the Shabbos urn keeping the water hot for my mother's tea.

"Wanna do Lego with me?" Max asks me, reappearing in his space ranger costume.

"Maybe when I get back," I say, slipping on my sandals.

CHAPTER 4

DEB?

"Milla!" Honey cries four days later when she spies me entering the schoolyard with Max and my mom.

I take off like a shot toward her. "Yay, you're here!" We hug, jumping up and down together in excitement.

"It's not fair," Max protests as he and my mother join us. "I finally get to kindergarten, but I still won't see you!" The middle school is in a different building from the nursery and the elementary school.

"We'll see each other when I get home," I say.

Dan-Dan yanks at Honey's skirt. Her two small ponytails look like a matching pair of trees on top of her head.

"Don't worry, I'll come visit you," Honey tells her, bending down to Dan-Dan's height and giving her a squeeze. "You too," she tells Aaron, who is wearing noise-canceling headphones, so I don't think he can hear her. She holds out a closed hand for their special fist bump, and he closes his own hand and lightly taps his fist onto hers.

Miriam is standing with her arms crossed and addresses the air in front of her. "You can force me to come here, but you can't force me to like it." She scowls even more gruesomely. "*Or* make any friends."

"You'll be just fine," Mrs. Wine tells her firmly, patting her shoulder. "Don't worry, you'll all be fine."

"I'm not worried," Honey says.

"C'mon," I say to her with a smile, giving my mother and Max a quick wave goodbye and leading Honey to the back where the middle school entrance is.

As we turn the corner, there is a scream.

"Honeeey!" Natalie Aronovich cries, rushing forward. "Oh my god, I'm so excited you're in our school now!" I roll my eyes to Honey, but she can't see because Natalie is crushing her in a hug. Honestly, the only reason Natalie even knows Honey is from my birthday parties.

"Hi, Milla! Hi, Honey!" Sophie Teischman and Tali Mandelcorn skip over and we group hug. In school, me, Sophie, Tali, and Natalie are kind of a loose foursome, although Sophie and Tali are best friends, and Natalie and I have a trickier relationship. Basically, sometimes she's great, and sometimes she really gets on my nerves.

"Hey, give us a turn!" Sophie says, nudging Natalie, who's posing for selfies with Honey.

I finally got my first phone just before I went to camp, but it's in my bag, switched off, per my mother's strict instructions. The rule for middle schoolers is that you can bring a phone to school, but it has to be off on school property. Honey extracts herself from Natalie's duck poses, again missing my conspiratorial eye roll, and takes turns hugging Sophie and Tali, who go to the same sleepaway camp as us. Natalie hovers over them. I *told* my mother everyone would love Honey!

Noam Cantor catches my eye from where he's standing with a group of boys and shouts, "Hi, Milla!"

"Hi!" I shout back with a wave. I am debating going over to him when he grabs Eitan Moses, who has grown the length of a ruler over the summer, and heads toward me.

"How was your summer?" I say.

"Great. Is that your friend Honey Wine?" Noam says, continuing past me to where Honey's excitedly chatting with Natalie, Sophie, and Tali.

Honey hears her name and glances up. "Who wants to know?" she challenges, winking at me. I adjust my knapsack on my shoulder and look at Noam.

"You're Ezra Wine's sister, right?" he says to Honey. He shakes his head in admiration. "Your brother is a sick athlete."

"Yeah, sick," Eitan chimes in.

"He was our counselor this summer," Noam continues. "I'm Noam, by the way . . ."

"Hey," Honey says nonchalantly.

Just then the bell rings, and we all gather at the entrance to squeeze our way in. The crowd surges forward, and suddenly I find myself at the back, seventh graders jostling me from every side. I can see Honey at the front, her arm linked with Natalie's.

Honey turns around to see where I am. "Milla?" she calls.

"Don't worry, I'm right behind you!" I holler over people's heads.

"I'm not worried," she calls back as she sails through the door.

Of course she isn't.

Our first class is Chumash, studying the Torah and its commentaries, and we have Mrs. Griswald, or rather Giveret Griswald. She is Israeli and speaks to us in Hebrew, regardless of whether or not we understand what she's saying.

She takes attendance, and when she gets to the last name on the list, she pauses and frowns. "What is 'Honey'?" she says in Hebrew.

"I'm Honey," says Honey in English, raising her hand.

"Ivrit b'vakashah," says Giveret Griswald, insisting on Hebrew.

"Ani Honey," says Honey.

"No, no, no," says Giveret Griswald in Hebrew. "Honey is not a name. And for certain it is not a name in Hebrew. What is your Hebrew name?"

I grimace. Honey is quiet.

Honey's real name is not even Honey. It's Hencha. That's her Jewish name anyway. She is named after her great-grandmother and no one expected her to be called Hencha (lucky for her!), but then they were too busy to come up with another name and just took to calling her Honey. She once showed me her birth certificate: It says "Baby Girl Wine."

Everyone in our class is staring at Honey, waiting for her to answer. She doesn't look worried exactly—her chin is high and her blond ponytail is steady—but her ears have turned red. She catches my eye, and I nod ever so slightly back to say, "Don't worry, the sound of 'Hencha' will never leave my lips."

I forgot to warn her that in our school the Judaic Studies teachers call you by your Hebrew name—whether you like it or not. Tali Mandelcorn is still Tali, which is short for Talia, Noam Cantor is still Noam, and Eitan Moses is still Eitan. But Ethans T. and W. are also Eitan, although Ethan S. is Eliezer. I, unfortunately, am Rut, the Hebrew for my middle name, Ruth, and pronounced "root." I hate it!

I look up to see Natalie giving Honey a reassuring, sympathetic look.

Honey turns a stony gaze back to Giveret Griswald.

"Ani *Honey*," she says again, not giving an inch.

Giveret Griswald clicks her tongue in annoyance. "Okay, ehhh, honey is dvash in Hebrew, but Dvash?—no! Dvash is not a name either. Ahhhhh, but what makes the honey? A bee—a devorah. Here we will call you Devorah. A beautiful name."

I brace myself: I'm worried sparks are

about to fly. For sure Honey is not going to back down.

"Beseder," Honey says with a shrug.

Fine? I look at her sharply. It's true she doesn't really have a choice, but knowing Honey, I cannot believe she's giving in so easily. Except that with each class after, when the teacher calls out Honey Wine on the attendance sheet and asks for her Hebrew name, she promptly supplies "Devorah."

"I'm so sorry, I forgot to warn you about the Hebrew name," I say when we are dismissed for recess. "I can't believe you're now Devorah!" I scrunch my face.

Honey smiles. "Don't worry, Milla. No big deal. It's like your Aunty Steph always says, 'Lemonade out of lemons,' right?"

"If you say so," I say, relieved that she's not mad at me. I guess there's nothing wrong with Devorah as long as Honey thinks it's okay. But I also feel a little twinge of unfairness. Why do I have to be Rut? Who knew you could just change your name?

After lunch, we return to a different classroom, and Mrs. McIntosh, the math teacher, takes attendance. "Honey Wine?" she calls toward the end of the list. Honey raises her hand.

"Actually, my name is Deborah," she says. "But you can call me Debbie."

I cough.

I look over and expect to share a smirk, but Honey doesn't notice. She's watching Mrs. McIntosh scribbling numbers on the whiteboard. I try to catch her eye the rest of the class, but Honey doesn't turn around once—she's too busy participating! It turns out Honey is really good at math, my weakest subject.

Finally, the bell rings. Mrs. McIntosh saunters out, and Mr. Sandler strides in for English.

"So, kids," he says. Everyone settles down right away. I notice Noam Cantor sitting up a bit straighter. Mr. Sandler holds up the attendance sheet. "You're all here, yes? First day of school and all?"

I feel my spirits lift. Mr. Sandler has a reputation for being the best teacher in the middle school. And English is my best subject. "All right, let's forget this, then." He hands the attendance clipboard to shy Rivkie Feuerstein, sitting in the center of the front row, and tells her to tick off everyone's names. Her eyes get even bigger when he gives her a pen from behind his ear. Everyone laughs.

"Okay, great. That's out of the way. Now let's talk about this year." He holds his hand over his eyes like he's the captain of a ship, staring off into the distance. He swivels to scan the classroom. I look around: I'm definitely not the only one who is holding their breath in anticipation.

"So, sixth grade. It's a big year. You're all going to grow up a lot by June. Trust me. Most of it is not going to be in ways that will have anything to do with me teaching you about the English language and its literature. But"—he raps his hand against Rivkie's desk and she jumps—"in case you're curious, we are going to learn poetry, we are going to learn grammar, we are going to learn about heroes and how ordinary people can do extraordinary things. We—actually, *you*—are going to write a speech and perform it in front of your whole class. Maybe in front of the whole school."

I realize I am still holding my breath, hanging on his words. I love English. And I can already tell I'm going to love having Mr. Sandler as my teacher.

"All right," Mr. Sandler says. "Now, everyone make yourself a name card and put it on your desk for the first few days so I know who's giving me the good answers." He hands out white card stock to be passed back along the lines of desks. "Think about how you present yourselves. And remember, it's always good to be creative."

Everyone gets busy. I use my new highlighters to draw some flowers around my name. As I color, I think about the fact that I will have to write and present two speeches this year—one for English and one for my bat mitzvah. I stop coloring and see that my flowers look like cabbages. I turn around to check what Tali's doing. She's drawn a curlicue border with tulips and roses filling the space around her name. I fold my card in half so it sits on my desk like Mr. Sandler showed us and lean over to see if Honey's finished yet. Then my eyes bug out of their sockets.

In bold black marker, Honey has written her name. But she hasn't written Honey.

Or Hencha.

Or Devorah.

Not even Debbie.

She has written Deb.

Deb?

I snort with laughter.

"Psst," I try to catch her attention. "Psst," I say again louder. Honey turns to me, and I mouth, "Ha-ha-ha," pointing to her name card and making a silly face.

"Excuse me," Mr. Sandler booms, striding toward our desks. "Excuse me—Milla," he says reading my name card. "And—Deb," he says, reading hers. My stomach drops.

"I love jokes, and it seems you two have one about the name cards. Care to share?"

He waits expectantly. My face heats with shame, and I shake my head mutely.

"Milla thinks what I've done with my name card is funny," Honey says calmly, even though the tips of her ears are pink again.

"Is it?" Mr. Sandler asks.

"Not really," she says.

"Okay, so then we won't laugh," he says. "Names are very sensitive. Lots of emotional baggage in names."

I want to sink into the metal chair like a lump of putty. I feel a swelling in my throat, and I know that tears are brimming just behind my eyes.

"All right, kids," Mr. Sandler says, striding back to the front of the classroom. "Don't worry, we'll have lots of time for good jokes, good ideas, and good work this year."

I swallow. Honey stays facing forward in front of me, her back straight, paying rapt attention to Mr. Sandler. If writing Deb on her name card wasn't some kind of joke, then what was it?

"Deb?" I splutter as we wait in line to get on the bus, raising my eyebrows all the way up. "I don't get it. Your name is *Honey*."

"What's there not to get? Now it's Deb." She shrugs like this is no big deal.

"But your name is Honey," I repeat helplessly. "You're *Honey Wine*."

"Honestly, Milla, who names their kid after a kind of alcohol?" She shakes her head.

I just look at her. I never knew her name bothered her. Well, sure, Hencha might. But what's wrong with the name Honey?

"Anyway, it's not even like Honey is my real name," she continues when she sees I have no response. "And the only proof I'm Hencha is that that's what my father named me when he was called to the Torah on the Shabbos after I was born. You've seen my birth certificate: My parents couldn't be bothered to name me, so why shouldn't I name myself?"

I feel like it probably isn't worth mentioning that it's essentially Giveret Griswald who has named her.

"Bye, Deb!" Natalie Aronovich calls from an open window of a sports car driving past us.

"See you, Nat!" Honey calls back with a wave and a smile. *"What?"* she says to me in response to my look.

"Nothing," I say quietly, kicking a stone with my toe.

"How was school?" Mom asks the second I walk in the door from the bus stop. *How'd it go?* my dad texts me. I get messages from Aunty Steph and both my grandmothers—the one who lives in Miami and the one who lives in Israel—asking me the same thing.

"Fine," I tell everyone, but when Max asks me at dinner if my first day of sixth grade was as exciting as his first day of kindergarten, I snap, "It's complicated, Max. You wouldn't understand." Then I stare into my bowl of pasta and try to ignore the hurt look on his face. After dinner, I go upstairs, drag my desk chair over to my closet, and take down my bin of dolls.

I don't consider it babyish that I still play with them sometimes, even though I don't tell anyone about it in case they think it is. But tonight I don't even make up sophisticated scenarios or dress them for an event. I just brush and brush their hair, like I used to when I was in kindergarten.

The next afternoon, when Mr. Sandler walks in, he hands out photocopies of a poem and asks us to read it to ourselves a few times. The class goes quiet with concentration. I look at the poem—it's short and seems simple, about a red wheelbarrow left out in the rain, and how much depends on it.

"So," Mr. Sandler says after a few minutes. "What do you think this poem is trying to tell us?"

I frown. What *is* it about? The whole poem is only sixteen words, but I suddenly suspect there is something deeper behind each word. I keep my hands in my lap. I don't want to say something stupid.

No one else is raising their hand either.

"Anyone care to take a stab?" Mr. Sandler asks.

It's very quiet. Something flashes through my head. I raise my hand tentatively.

"Yes, Milla?" He doesn't need to see my name

card. He remembers it from yesterday. I take a deep breath.

"Um, well, little things can be important?"

"Okay. Can you say more?" Mr. Sandler asks. He's looking at me with interest.

"Well, people say, 'Don't sweat the small stuff,' but sometimes small details are really important and can make all the difference. We don't know why the red wheelbarrow is important, or why so much depends on the red wheelbarrow, but we know that it is important to someone, and that someone feels that everything depends on it. Maybe?"

"*Very* nice, Milla," Mr. Sandler says. I try to suck in my cheeks so no one can see that I'm smiling too obviously. It's hard.

"Okay, that's great," he says to the rest of the class, rubbing his hands together. "Now, what do you make of how the poem is built? What might the poet, William Carlos Williams, be trying to tell us by how he constructed each sentence?" It gets very quiet. People have their heads down again, trying to scrutinize the poem.

"Be braaaave," Mr. Sandler says in a spooky movie voice. "No . . . wrong . . . opinions." Everyone laughs a bit, but no one raises their hand. I take another deep breath and raise mine, all the way up this time.

"Go for it, Milla," he says.

"Um, so, each line is three words and then has a line after it of one word. And the one word continues the sentence *and* kind of changes the meaning of the line before it."

Mr. Sandler is nodding excitedly and moving his hand as if to say "and . . . ?"

"Well, the poem starts with the words 'so much depends,' and really everything depends on each word of the poem because it's so short so every word has meaning and importance. Especially even the smallest, single word."

"Excellent again, Milla." His grin is infectious, and his eyes are sparkling.

I can feel my face getting flushed. It is hard to stop the smile from spreading up to my ears.

"Anyone else?" he says. One hand goes up. It's Honey's. "Deb?" he calls on her, remembering her name too.

"Yeah, like Milla said, everything depends on everything, whether it's small or big, everything in life is connected."

"That's beautiful, Deb."

Honey beams and turns around to catch my eye. I smile back. But I can't help feeling like I am a birthday balloon from three days ago, still shiny but no longer floating up to the ceiling. English is *my* best subject. Math is *hers*.

CHAPTER 5

A ROSE BY ANY OTHER NAME

By the time Friday afternoon comes around, I have been in middle school for a total of three days and I am thoroughly worn out. I always thought the older I got the more I would stay up late, but now I understand why Josh Wine goes to sleep right after dinner on Friday nights. Being more grown-up is exhausting. I can't wait for Shabbat.

Honey has saved a seat for me on the bus, and I flop down beside her.

"Nat invited me to come over on Sunday," she tells me.

"Cool," I say, feigning a smile. "Her house is really nice. They have an indoor swimming pool."

"Yeah, she told me to bring a bathing suit." Honey shrugs.

I know she doesn't really care how fancy or big someone's house is or isn't. But I wonder if Natalie knows she can't just buy Honey's friendship.

"She's nice," Honey says, giving me a look. "She's gone out of her way to make me feel welcome."

"Great," I say, until I realize what Honey's said. "Wait, who's not making you feel welcome?"

She's quiet for a minute. Then she turns to me. "Milla, why aren't you calling me Deb? Everyone is except for you."

She means *I'm* not making her feel welcome? "Oh, like your new bestie, Nat?" I say before I can help myself.

She raises her eyebrows. "You don't see me making a big deal about you signing up to do Mr. Hill's geography project with Sophie and Tali."

I flush guiltily. It's true. I'd immediately signaled to Sophie and Tali; the three of us always work on assignments together. But by the time it occurred to me to include Honey, Natalie had already pulled her chair over to Honey's desk.

"You could have joined us if you wanted to," I say.

She raises her eyebrows again to let me know she doesn't buy it, but all she says is, "I like Natalie, but you're my best friend, Milla." She looks away.

I shrug. I know that. But all the feelings of the last few days come to the surface and I can't lie to her. "It just feels like everyone is trying to take you over!"

"Excuse me," she says, sitting up straighter and

jutting out her chin. "But no one is taking me over. No one takes over Honey Wine. I mean Deb Wine."

"Yeah, and that's the other thing," I say. "It just feels really . . . unlike you to change your name just because a teacher told you to."

"Why do you care what I call myself?" she says. "And may I remind you of your Starbucks name, *Cami*?"

"It's Camille," I say. "And anyway, that's totally different."

"Why?" she shoots back. "Why is that different?"

I search for what to say. It just feels different, Starbucks and school.

"You're—" I start. "It's like you're taking the opportunity of being in a new school to change your name and be a different person."

"Well, I'm not a different person. I'm me. And I like who I am." Honey pulls her legs up to sit cross-legged on the seat. I shift over, to avoid her knee jutting into me. "Why would changing my name make me a different person?"

I don't have an answer. We ride the rest of the way home in silence.

When I get home, Aunty Steph has just arrived, and I give her a big hug.

"Milla-babe," she says, hugging me back for a really long time, enveloping me in the smell of lavender and body odor that is uniquely Aunty Steph.

"Your mom's just dropped off Max and me and gone to run some errands," she says. "Come, let's hang out." She hefts her huge camping knapsack onto one shoulder and climbs the stairs to the spare room across from Max's bedroom, where she sleeps whenever she stays with us.

Max is in the bathroom peeing with the door open. "If it's yellow, let it mellow, right, Maxie?" she calls to him. Aunty Steph works at a retreat center in the forest for people who want to learn about Judaism and the environment. When she pees, she doesn't flush the toilet so as not to waste water.

"You got it, Aunty Steph!" he says. He loves this rule for some reason. I should know. I share a bathroom with him. I think it's gross, so I always flush. But I still think Aunty Steph is the coolest. She's my mom and uncles' baby sister and was only a teenager when I was born, so it feels more like she's an older sister to me than an aunt.

Aunty Steph drops her bag on the floor with a thump and lies down on the bed, indicating to me that I should do the same on the massage table. There isn't a whole lot of room in here. When my parents bought this house, I think they imagined this would be another kid's bedroom, but that didn't work out. And when I said that everything in our house is "just so," in perfect order, all the time, I should have added that there is one exception: this room, which is "just so . . . messy."

All around me are bags of my and Max's old clothes, files from my mom's old job, including her framed diplomas, certificates, and awards, and all kinds of questionable keepsakes—like Uncle Dougie's old hockey card collection and Uncle Robbie's wrestling dolls—that used to be in my grandmother's house until she downsized and moved to Miami. My dad says this is a room filled with stuff my mom doesn't want to give away but that serves no practical purpose whatsoever. Except for the massage table from when Aunty Steph thought she would be a massage therapist—sometimes my dad uses it as an ironing board. And now I'm lying on it.

"Okay, Milla-babe, fill me in. How's school so far?"

"Fine," I say.

She's lying on her back too. "Just 'fine'?" I can hear the smile in her voice.

It feels surprisingly serene to stare at the ceiling. I take a deep breath. And then I find myself telling her everything that's been going on this week.

". . . Honey coming to my school just hasn't been what I expected," I conclude, finally coming up for air.

"It sounds like Honey calling herself Deb is really bothering you," Aunty Steph says.

"Well, it's like, why does she get to change her name?"

Aunty Steph nods.

"And everyone is going along with it. Why do I have to be Rut?"

"So, do you want to change your name too? What would you change it to?"

"Well—" This stops me in my tracks. I shift on the massage table. I have no idea what I would change my Hebrew name to if I had the choice. It never occurred to me that it was up to me.

"Milla-babe," Aunty Steph says gently after a minute. I turn onto my side and look at her. She sits up and crosses her legs, swiveling so her back leans against the wall and she's facing me. "It won't serve you well on your life's journey to be jealous of Honey. She's her and you're you. You need to own who you are."

"Who said anything about jealous?" I say.

Aunty Steph doesn't say anything in response. I turn onto my back to look at the ceiling again. I feel disgruntled and more confused than ever. After a few minutes, I shift onto my side to see if Aunty Steph has fallen asleep.

Sensing my shift, she opens her eyes and smiles at me. "I think you're right that sometimes people change their names because they want to be a different person," she says. "Or sometimes a different name just feels more like how they see themselves. People have their own reasons for changing their name. Reasons that are personal to them. It's not for us to judge."

I turn onto my stomach and look through the doughnut hole at the top of the massage table. A picture of my mother as her high school valedictorian is right underneath me. I realize that what Honey said on the bus—about liking herself—is true. She never worries if she's going to look silly or that people will laugh at her or that her clothes aren't that fashionable. Unlike me, she just does what feels right.

The door swings open, and Max appears in his space ranger costume holding a thin book in his hand. "Wanna see my first reading book, Aunty Steph? Will you read it with me? Milla, you can listen."

Max climbs into Aunty Steph's lap and slowly sounds out the simple words in his reader. I look at his dark hair pressing against the hood of his costume. Even though my mother washes it several times a week, the whole jumpsuit is filthy.

"Why do you wear your costumes all the time, Max?" I say, interrupting him from Biff and Muff, who have a dog they pat.

Max looks up from his reader. "Because I like it."

"But why?" I press. He looks at me blankly. I can see he doesn't understand my question.

Aunty Steph smiles at me significantly. "Milla-babe, isn't that he likes it reason enough?"

On the playground Monday before school, Natalie and I are wall ball captains, and it is my turn to choose first.

"Deb!" I say, calling Honey to my team before Natalie gets a chance.

Honey raises her eyebrows at me and then flashes me a wide smile. "Changed my mind," she calls. "I'm back to Honey."

"What?" I say.

"I'm Honey again," she says.

"You are?" I ask, surprised.

"You sure?" Natalie echoes, even more surprised than me as Honey skips over to stand with me.

"Yup, everyone, call me Honey!"

And I don't know if Honey privately spoke to all the teachers or Mrs. Wine telephoned the school, but from that day on Honey is called Hencha in the mornings and Honey in the afternoons. With the exception of Giveret Griswald, who pretends she doesn't understand Honey's English and insists on calling her Devorah, while Honey pretends she doesn't understand Giveret Griswald's Hebrew and doesn't respond.

On the bus home that day though, I ask Honey what made her change her mind.

She shrugs. "I didn't think anyone had ever put

any thought into my name, chosen it for *me*. You know?"

"I guess so," I say, thinking of Rut. I mean, my parents chose it because I was born just before the festival of Shavuot, when the Book of Ruth—Megillat Rut—is read in synagogue. But what does it really have to do with *me*?

"But then Abba told me about my great-grandmother Hencha—not the one whose house we have, the other one—Abba's grandmother. And he showed me a picture. He said that she was a really cool and strong-willed lady. She was blond and didn't look Jewish, but instead of going into hiding from the Nazis with a non-Jewish family, she chose to stay and help her mother with her younger siblings. And then got sent to a concentration camp with them." Honey's smattering of freckles have deepened, and she fingers the ends of her own blond ponytail thoughtfully. "Only she survived."

We're both quiet.

"I'm sorry for not calling you Deb if that's what you wanted," I say finally. "And . . . I'm sorry if I wasn't more welcoming."

"That's okay," Honey says. "I wasn't worried . . . But

thanks for saying that." She says the last bit in a rush. Then she grins impishly. "Anyway, being Deb was fun for a while, but Honey's way better for me. Honestly, *who* else in the world is called Honey Wine?"

"Just my best friend," I say.

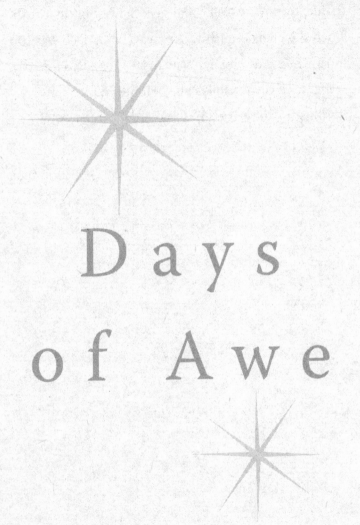

Days
of Awe

CHAPTER 6

AGINÉNI

"She's so mean," I say. We are in the Wines' front yard, and Honey is putting covered foil tins into a faded navy-blue stroller so that we can walk the food over to Aginéni's. It's the day before Rosh Hashanah, the Jewish New Year, and school has ended early with no homework because of the holiday, so I came back to Honey's. But then Mrs. Wine told Honey she needs her to deliver food to Aginéni so she'll have a stocked fridge for the holiday.

"Oh, she's so sweet. She's cute," Honey says, accidentally pushing the stroller away as she tries to slide in the heavy tin of brisket. I raise my eyebrows and roll the stroller back to her, holding it steady while she carefully places the apple kugel on top of the brisket.

All the kids in our neighborhood know Aginéni for a few reasons. One of them being that she drives herself around in a little red car honking at all the kids playing hockey or hopscotch in the crescent in front of Honey's house. She doesn't like to back her car out into oncoming traffic, so instead she makes three right turns to get onto Honey's street. Then she drives around the half circle, her fist on the horn, scattering sticks, cracking Hula-Hoops, and breaking fat pieces of chalk before she's finally back in the direction she came from and ready to make her left turn.

Aginéni is not a sweet, old grandma type, and this is the main reason she is very well known.

"Shhhhh!" Aginéni will say in shul if a child dares whine or ask their mother or father for something. "Vilde chaya," she'll add, muttering about kids who behave without any decorum—all this from her front-row balcony seat, where she can keep an eye on both the ladies' section *and* the main sanctuary down below. On the rare occasion Aginéni is late to shul on Shabbat, woe to the unsuspecting person who has plopped herself down in what appeared to be an available seat. After a hard rap on the shoulder, no one ever makes the same mistake again.

"I'm not scared of an old lady," Honey says as she finishes loading the food and crosses her arms. "Anyway, we can put in for community service points." So far, Honey is winning in our class. Honey likes to win at things, and this is an easy one for her.

"Shnorrer," I say, telling her she's being grubby, another one of Aginéni's favorites.

"Farbissineh!" she says, telling me I'm acting like Miriam.

"Vilde chaya!" we shriek at the same time, and then growl at each other before we both burst out laughing.

"Race you!" says Honey. Then she's off, swerving into the walking path, speed walking over the hardened mud, and as we emerge onto my street and turn left toward Aginéni's, running wildly, pushing the old broken carriage down the street, me at her heels.

When we get to Aginéni's, we are totally out of breath. Honey rings the bell while I start bringing the tinfoil pans up the broken cement steps to the porch. She rings again, and we wait, leaning against the wrought iron railing. Finally, the scrunched-together curtain on the narrow window surrounding the door is pulled aside and a nose pushes against the glass. The door opens, and there is Aginéni.

Instead of her usual groomed wig, Aginéni's head is covered in a faded pink turban, and she is wearing a pilled and shredded pink housecoat. I suddenly realize I haven't seen her in shul in a long time.

She glances at Honey in recognition, and then she looks at me with curiosity. I know who she is, of course, but even if she *might* recognize me as a shul kid, she doesn't know who I am other than one of the Wine daughters' friends. I grip the edges of the pan tightly and offer a shaky smile.

"Nu, come in already," she commands, shuffling slowly out of the way to let us by.

She is stooped over. Her face is bony, and her eyes are dark and watery. When I watch her move slowly toward her kitchen while we lug the food after her, something starts softly tapping on my heart.

"Aginéni, you want me to paint your nails?" Honey says, settling her pans on the counter. The stove and fridge are turquoise, and the brown-and-white linoleum floor is curling in some places. "I do it for all the ladies I visit at Zonnenshein Home."

As I put my pan next to Honey's, I grin at the mental image of Aginéni getting a manicure from Honey, but also wonder not for the first time how Honey has the guts to address grown-ups by their names. Even Mrs. Wine—Judy—I don't actually call her anything. If I need to ask her something, I just awkwardly clear my throat or say "um" until she looks up.

"What, you think I'm ready for the alte kaker house and I'm going to sing tra-la-la while you do my nails because I don't have a thought left in my head?" Aginéni looks at Honey with venom. "Don't do me any favors with your foolish nahrishkeit."

Honey scowls and exhales loudly through her nose. Then she turns her back to Aginéni and stalks toward the oven.

There is something so funny about how Honey thought she was going to tame Aginéni. To stop myself from laughing, I look out the window, opened a crack to let in a sliver of fresh air. The backyard is ravaged by weeds and overgrown plants. Even though it is almost fall and getting chilly, I don't get the feeling that it looked any better in the spring or summer. But then I glimpse a single pink rose on a bush at the side of the house. It looks like it has been gently placed there by a fairy in the night, perfect and still blooming.

Honey turns on the sink, and the sound pulls my gaze back inside. My eyes catch the sheen off the plastic cover of a library book resting on the island between the main part of the kitchen and the little eating area. I can't believe it. It's *Most Likely To . . . Rion*, the first book in my absolute favorite series of all time.

"Are you reading this?" I ask Aginéni before I can stop myself. The series is about a group of kids working on their high school yearbook, and each book is from a different character's perspective. My mom thinks it's a little old for me because there's kissing and other stuff, and she says the topics can be a little "heavy," but I love these books so much I don't care. Plus, that's what makes them so good. You really feel like the author, R. S. Williams, *gets* teenagers, and kids, and what people are really like. "I love this series!" I say, and it comes out like a squeak.

"And what if I am reading it?" Aginéni replies. "An old lady should sit at home by herself all day staring at the walls? I used to knit, but look—" She holds out her fingers, gnarled to claws. "And they took my license away after I didn't pass their farkakteh test."

I nod. I guess I haven't seen her driving around recently either.

"So I go to the library once a week with the Elder-Trans and I load up. The librarian, she already knows me. She gives me recommendations." She ticks them off on her crooked fingers. "May Magus, Helly Simpson, Jay Schwartz—now R. S. Williams." She points to the book on the island. "Children's, adult, even young adult. I read it all!"

I try to memorize the names of the other authors she says she reads so I can look them up when I get home. If she's reading Most Likely To . . . then Aginéni has good taste in books.

"Why do you read *kids'* books?" Honey says, turning off the sink and wiping her hands on a threadbare dish towel. A clean glass mug and some spoons are now sitting in the drainboard.

"And why shouldn't I?" Aginéni says haughtily, narrowing her eyes at Honey. "Are you saying I am an old lady and should be banned from reading what I want to? The alte kakers can only read the boring stuff?"

"Um, you're not old, Aginéni," Honey mutters as Aginéni dares her with her eyes. I have to hold back the urge to laugh again and instead try to rescue my friend.

"Just wait till you get to the third book in the series," I say. "And the fourth one is my favorite. I was so mad at Daisy for what she did to Ellen in the one you're reading, but then, in the fourth, it's Daisy's side and you find out why she was keeping secrets."

Aginéni shoots another chilly glance at Honey and then looks at me brightly. "You see? Very mature ideas in books for children. Just look at Ella Draggon-Hart. Those books are all about the Nazis!" She makes a spitting sound.

I start in surprise and wonder if that is true. Yezer *is* very evil. I look out the window again for a minute so that I don't look at Aginéni's arm even though it is covered. Another thing all the neighborhood kids know about Aginéni is that she has a number on her arm because she is a survivor from the Holocaust.

"Ella Draggon-Hart is not about the Nazis!" protests Honey. "It's fantasy."

"Have *you* read it?" asks Aginéni.

"No, but—"

"Then, what do you know?"

"Well, I've seen the movies." Honey scowls.

"So nu, what's Daisy's secret?" Aginéni asks me.

"I don't want to spoil it," I say.

"Oh, just spit it out," Aginéni commands.

I take a gulp. "She's been meeting with her grandmother." Aginéni's eyes widen. Daisy is a Jewish character. Her parents grew up Hasidic but left their sect before she was born and now don't keep any

Jewish laws or customs. Her dad even fries bacon for breakfast! In butter! Eating pork and mixing meat with dairy is as non-kosher as you can get. And they don't have anything to do with her grandparents, who won't talk to her family and have disowned them.

"I knew it!" Aginéni says with a satisfied smile. "You see, Hakadosh Baruch Hu works in mysterious ways." She points her finger to the ceiling, talking about God. Honey picks up the book and starts scanning the back cover. "That Daisy has a Yiddishe neshama no matter her parents' own choices," Aginéni says.

Aginéni means that Daisy has a "Jewish soul." Daisy's parents so badly want her to have a "normal" life and not the ultra-Orthodox one they grew up in, where they always had to hold themselves separate from the rest of the world. But Daisy goes searching for her roots because she doesn't know what it means to be Jewish, and she *wants* to feel a part of something and understand where she comes from.

To be honest, until I read Most Likely To . . . it was something I hadn't even thought about before. Maybe because almost everyone I know is religious, and being Modern Orthodox, we observe the laws like keeping Shabbat and keeping kosher, but we also go to college, have jobs, and *are* part of modern life. The series made me realize that being religious guides everything I do—from what I eat, to what I wear, to where I go to school. Sure, when I see kids on TV, I realize that my life is a little different. But in other ways it feels a lot the same—especially inside. Where it matters.

"I guess," I say finally, feeling like it's complicated.

Honey has put the book down and is pulling a long strand of her hair in and out of her mouth. She's not a reader.

"Okay, girls," says Aginéni, drawing her hand to the hip of her pink housecoat. "As my dear husband, Imre-batchi, used to say: 'Guests are like fish, they start to stink.'"

"That's after three days!" Honey retorts, her body jutting forward.

"Tell your mother she's a tzadeikis," she says to Honey, which is not the first time I've heard Mrs. Wine called a righteous woman. "And I don't know who your mother is," Aginéni says to me, "but I'm glad she has a daughter who likes to read books. Come back and visit sometime. With this one"—she nods to Honey—"or without." She raises her eyebrows at me.

"A Gut Yor, girls," she rasps, wishing us Happy New Year in Yiddish.

"Shanah Tovah," we say to the back of her house-coat, wishing her the same in Hebrew.

As we pass by her cane on our way out, I think it kind of looks like a shofar, the ram's horn blown on Rosh Hashanah to awaken the congregation to repentance. I try to think of things I am sorry for, or that I want to do differently this year. Maybe I really could come back and visit Aginéni—I could bring her books. Everyone wants to be a better person, I think. Sometimes it's just hard.

"I thought you were scared of her," Honey says peevishly as soon as the screen door bangs shut behind us.

"I thought I was," I say. Then I smile mischievously. "I thought you weren't."

"I'm not!" she scoffs. Then *she* smiles mischievously. "Don't you give me that nahrishkeit!" She sprints down the porch steps and grabs the stroller.

"Vilde chaya!" I call, racing after her.

"Alte kaker!" she calls, waiting for me to catch up.

"Tra-la-la!" we sing at the same time, and then we run back to Honey's house laughing all the way home.

CHAPTER 7
SUCC⦿T

On the day after Yom Kippur, we have a middle school assembly right after morning prayers.

"Succot is the festival of insecurity," the speaker begins in a British accent, although Rabbi Adler introduced her as being from Israel. We only have school today and tomorrow before it closes for the eight days of Succot, and the auditorium is buzzing about who fasted on Yom Kippur, and what people ate to break their fasts, and plans for the festival next week.

"On Succot, we are celebrating and remembering when the Children of Israel lived in the desert on the way to the Promised Land—we lived in temporary huts, exposed to the elements," she carries on calmly, despite the thrum of whispers and giggles. "We had no idea if we would get to the Promised Land—what it looked like, if we would be successful there, or if it even existed."

She's wearing a suit with an elegant silk scarf knotted at her neck and a smaller silk scarf holding back her dark brown hair. I study the way she speaks to her audience—looking around the room in a practiced and confident way.

"Succot is like the years of adolescence—like being a *teenager*." She says the last part in a flawless American accent and then smiles as everyone laughs. She waits a beat before continuing, knowing that the whole auditorium is paying attention to her now. I see that Mr. Sandler—who, like the other general studies teachers, tends to mark assignments during Judaic Studies assemblies—has looked up, intrigued. I edge forward in my seat.

"Succot is the festival of insecurity. And you teenagers and soon-to-be teenagers—you are in a temporary dwelling right now, just like a succah. You know that adulthood exists; you even know actual adults."

I laugh appreciatively with everyone else. I like that she's being funny on her way to trying to tell us something meaningful.

"But you have no idea how it might exist for you, what it will look like." She glances at her notes before looking back up to meet our gazes. "Most nations don't like to be reminded of their humble origins, but the Jewish people's three pilgrimage festivals—Pesach,

Shavuot, and Succot—do just that. They are celebrations, but embedded within them is always a reminder of where we have come from and who we are."

I realize that my hands are making small motions in the air, following how she uses hers.

She adjusts her headscarf slightly and leans forward on the podium. "Embrace the things you can do to move yourself toward independence and the responsibilities that come with it. But also embrace the uncertainty, the insecurity, the time that you are taking to discover who you are."

"Discovah who yew ahhh," Natalie imitates, nudging me with her elbow, but I pretend I don't hear her.

In the afternoon, Mr. Sandler tells us to take out a fresh piece of paper.

"Pop creative writing assignment," he says. "I want you to take ten minutes and write about what insecurity means to you."

Honey raises her hand. "Can I write about food insecurity?"

I know the term from Aunty Steph, who took me to help at a soup kitchen last Thanksgiving, but there are lots of puzzled looks around me.

"Sure," Mr. Sandler says, nodding. Then he clarifies for the rest of the class: "You can write about insecurity in terms of food and shelter—not knowing where your next meal will come from or where you will sleep each night, and if it's safe. Or you can write about it in terms of feelings and emotions. Interpret it however you like."

What does insecurity mean to me? I write at the top of my page. Then I doodle a little on the side of the paper, in the margins. Then around my title. I color in the holes in the *o*'s. Then I do the *e*'s. Then the *a*'s. Everyone around me is busy scribbling away. I cover my paper with my hand so no one can see I haven't written anything. Normally I love creative writing assignments: I can fill sheets and sheets with my ideas and whenever the teacher says the time is up, I always feel I have more to say. But right now, I don't know where to begin. I look at Honey, her head bent over her paper in concentration, her ponytail falling to one side. *Mean to me*, I write again. *Mean to ME*, I write underneath it. *WHAT does it mean to me?* When the time is finally up, I fold my sheet in three and slide it into my notebook to throw away as soon as no one is looking.

"Milla, can you see me for a moment?" Mr. Sandler says. My heart sinks into my shoes and my face feels hot as I trudge over to the door, where he's beckoning me to meet him outside. "Writer's block?" he asks.

I nod. "Happens to the best of us," he says, leaning against the doorframe. "Don't worry, you'll do better next time."

I try to smile and realize with alarm that tears are crowding behind my eyes.

"And, Milla, everybody feels moments of insecurity—even adults." He smiles. "Some are just better at hiding it."

I nod. Then I swallow and find I am able to smile back now. Even though I have a feeling this may not be the last time I feel insecure about insecurity.

"Guess who's coming to dinner second night of Succot?" Honey says to me. It's Shabbat afternoon, and we're hanging out in the girls' bathroom upstairs at the Wine house.

"Who?" I say dramatically. It could literally be anybody.

"Naomi Dayan," she says, like I should know who that is.

"*Who?*" I say.

"You know, the speaker? From assembly?"

"Oh," I say, impressed.

"Her father's an Israeli diplomat and knows my grandfather." Honey shrugs. She doesn't think that stuff is a big deal. "Anyway, she's spending the year here teaching classes and giving lectures."

"Cool." I think about her confidence in speaking to an audience.

"Shmuel Yosef is going to be there too," Honey says. "At dinner, I mean."

"Who?" I say. "Oh, wait, do you mean Sam?"

"He prefers Shmuel Yosef now, Milla, so we should be respectful of his getting more religious."

"O-kay," I say, about to roll my eyes at her tone before I stop myself. "Good to know," I say instead. Sam—or Shmuel Yosef—is one of the Wines' hangers. But he is more memorable to the neighborhood kids than the others because of the motorcycle he vrooms through the streets and then leaves parked on the Wines' driveway all Shabbat so as not to break the laws of the Sabbath by riding home. All Saturday long, kids congregate around it like a magnet they cannot touch.

"What do you think of his beard?" Honey says.

"Um. I don't?" Beards are something I spend zero time thinking about.

"Really? I think it's so handsome." She rolls onto her back on the fuzzy yellow bathroom rug, avoiding my very-highly-raised eyebrows.

"I've been thinking about the speaker though," I tell her, deciding to file away Honey's slightly pink-turning face and her use of the word handsome.

"Me too," Honey says, rolling back toward me on the bathroom rug. "Do you want to come for dinner when she comes?"

"Aunty Steph is staying with us," I say, a bit regretfully.

"Okay." Honey shrugs. "By the way, do you know where Steph got her wraparound skirt?"

"*Steph?*" I say, raising my eyebrows again.

"She's not my aunt," Honey says. "Anyway, I was thinking I could use one like that to wear on Sundays."

"I think she goes to vintage shops," I say. Definitely something my mother wrinkles her nose about, no matter how much she loves her sister. Then I sit up straight. "Wait—could Aunty Steph come to dinner too?" I'm imagining me and Aunty Steph walking over to the Wines' together. Just us, without the rest of my family.

"Ooh, great idea!" Honey says. "I'll ask Ima, but I'm sure it's fine. Will *your* mom be okay with it?"

"I could tell Aunty Steph to ask. She never says no to her."

"Wait, I have the best idea!" Honey says. "Tell your mom that there'll be some eligible bachelors for your aunt to meet. I'm sure some random single bochers my dad is learning with will be there, so it's not even a lie. Didn't you say your mom is always trying to set her up? Steph's not getting any younger, you know."

"She's only twenty-five," I protest.

"And that is why she needs a shidduch, pronto," Honey says.

I nod. Well, my mom does think it's high time Aunty Steph started dating "men who are marriage material"—and not the "artsy-fartsy hippies" with whom Aunty Steph has a tendency for intense, short-lived relationships. Although I don't think that any of the people who end up at the Wines' are Aunty Steph's type, or what my mother would consider marriage material. But I *am* thinking about how much fun it would be to have my favorite aunt and my favorite family all together.

"You know I'm righ-ight," Honey singsongs with a playful grin, her eyes starting to cross and her finger inching toward her nose.

I roll my eyes at her antics. But despite my best intentions, the corners of my mouth start tugging up until we're both laughing hysterically.

"What's so funny in there?" Miriam bangs on the door.

"*Adolescent* stuff—aka none of your beeswax!" Honey hollers back.

On the second night of Succot, Aunty Steph and I plan to walk over to the Wines' together after she and my mom say the blessing on the candles. My mother lights the wicks while Aunty Steph sings a song without words, just *"lai-la-lai,"* and closes her eyes and sways. She puts one arm around me and one around my mother, and we move awkwardly like we are in a three-legged race. I join in with the humming and try not to get too impatient. Or think about our small canvas succah on the back porch and my mother's face as she set three lonely place settings huddled together at one end of the table.

"Your mom's asked me to learn with you for your

bat mitzvah," Aunty Steph says as we finally extract ourselves and head down my driveway.

"Cool!" I say. There are lots of things a girl can do in honor of her bat mitzvah, and for mine, my parents and I have already agreed that I'll study a Jewish text and do a mitzvah project for a charity. We'll have a party, and I'll make a speech, summarizing whatever I study. I give a little skip and hop on the sidewalk. I'm so glad my mom thought of asking Aunty Steph to learn with me!

"She thought we could study Megillat Rut together. Is that okay with you, Milla-babe?"

I try not to let my face fall. "Rut" again.

I sigh. I guess since I was born on the eve of Shavuot—the festival that the Book of Ruth is connected to—it does make sense to study it for my bat mitzvah.

"Sure," I say with a shrug. It is fall already, and the dark night has a crisp chill to it. As we approach the path that leads to Honey's street, the wind rushes through the bushes. It *is* exciting to be out, just me and Aunty Steph. She links her arm through mine.

"*We're* . . ." she begins, looking at me and holding one leg out.

I kick mine into a skip-hop like Aunty Steph taught me. *"Off to see the wizard, the wonderful Wizard of Oz!"* we sing together, our legs kicking in time.

"Because, because, because, because of the wonderful things he does!" we belt. It feels like a good way to get to the Wines'.

Honey greets us at the door before I even have a chance to knock. "Naomi Dayan just got here. She and her husband went to a different shul that ended already. But Shmuel Yosef is at our shul with Abba," she adds. "They'll be back soon."

"Chag Sameach, Sugaree," Aunty Steph says to Honey, wishing her a happy holiday and enveloping her in a characteristically long hug. Honey loves Aunty Steph's nickname for her, but I can sense her starting to squirm to be let out of the embrace.

"Aunty Steph," I say. "Naomi Dayan is the speaker I was telling you about."

"Right on," Aunty Steph says, releasing Honey. "And who's Shmuel Yosef?" she asks her with a smile.

"Shmuel Yosef is a photographer—like, that's his job. He says photography is all about light," Honey says.

"I agree." Aunty Steph smiles, unbuttoning her sweater coat and shaking out her hair, the smell of lavender floating over us. I remember that she studied photography as part of her thesis back when she was getting her masters in history.

Mrs. Wine looks up with her warm smile when we come into the living room, and she introduces everyone. I smile shyly at Naomi Dayan and her husband. I want Aunty Steph to talk to Naomi, but Susie is occupying her by trying to speak in baby-word Hebrew. Aaron comes in with Abbie, his therapist, who works with him three times a week no matter what, even on holidays. She asks him to look at each of us and say "Hello."

"Hello," he says to each person he walks up to, looking slightly past them.

"Hello, Aaron," I say when it's my turn, hoping he'll respond "Hello, Aaron" or even "Hello, Milla," because other than the Wines here, he knows me best. But he's moved on to Naomi Dayan.

"Pleased to meet you," she tells him elegantly, as if the Wines' living room was Buckingham Palace, and I see Honey giving her an appraising look of approval.

Then the rest of the Wines and their guests start

trooping in from shul, trailing through the house in their long navy woolen coats and hats and gloves, Shmuel Yosef in a leather motorcycle jacket.

"Gut Yontef!" everyone says, wishing each other a happy holiday.

The newly arrived stamp their feet to get some warmth back into them while we pile our own coats and hats and scarves on. Aunty Steph buttons her heavy knitted sweater coat back up. Naomi Dayan swoops a cape over her shoulders. I look down at the Shabbat winter coat my mother bought last fall. The velvet collar feels babyish.

"Steph, this is Shmuel Yosef," Honey introduces.

"You're the photographer," replies Aunty Steph. "Right on."

"Shmuel Yosef," he says, putting out his hand and then (glimpsing Mr. Wine slightly shaking his head) taking it back quickly; he leans forward instead and grins goofily at Aunty Steph.

Aunty Steph smiles.

Everyone crowds out the back door, where the Wines' wooden succah is erected over the entirety of their large tiled patio. Adorning every inch of wall space is years' worth of Wine kids' decorations. Yellow camping lights along with apples, gourds, and colored tinfoil hang from the ceiling—which actually isn't really a ceiling but bamboo sticks covered with leaves so that you can see the stars. I scan the place cards shaped like etrogs—the citron fruit that is one of the symbols of Succot—for my name; I recognize the handwriting as Honey's.

I am across from Shmuel Yosef, in between Miriam and Aunty Steph. Honey has placed herself one seat in, between Dan-Dan and Shmuel Yosef. As promised, both on Aunty Steph's other side and across from her are two random bochers I've never seen before. Naomi Dayan and her husband are all the way at the other end of the succah, not close enough to talk to.

"Hey, Milla, catch!" Micah calls after Hamotzi, shooting a challah crumb at me down the table.

I perk up and smile. "Right back at you!" I say, pretending to throw my whole slice of challah at him.

"Ow!" Miriam cries as my elbow accidentally connects with her head.

"Sorry!" I say sheepishly. Micah is silently laughing and pointing from the other end of the table.

"You okay?" Aunty Steph asks me and Miriam. I

nod. A smile plays at her lips as she leans over and rubs both our heads. *"Two worlds collided..."* she sings in her high-pitched voice.

"And they could never tear us apart..." Shmuel Yosef continues in a deep baritone.

"Never tear us apart," Aunty Steph and Shmuel Yosef repeat, singing together. I raise my eyebrows at Honey, but she's not looking at me. Her ears have turned red and she's staring at my aunt and Shmuel Yosef.

We eat steaming bowls of butternut squash soup, plump cabbage rolls, honey mustard brisket, and deep orange sweet potatoes. The smell of the apple crisp in the warming oven wafts through the succah every time the door to the kitchen is opened or closed. Everything is sweet. Except for Honey's face, which is souring by the minute. Aunty Steph does not seem to find the young men sitting next to or across from her very interesting. But she and Shmuel Yosef have been keeping up a steady stream of animated conversation throughout the meal.

Just before Grace After Meals, Mr. Wine asks Naomi Dayan to offer some words—a dvar Torah— about the holiday. She smiles, seemingly unfazed by being put on the spot like that.

I nudge Aunty Steph and whisper, "You'll see, she's good." Aunty Steph nods and turns to face her at the end of the table. Naomi Dayan thinks for a minute and then clears her throat.

"In order to perform the unique Succot mitzvah of lulav and etrog, where we take three plants bound together with a fruit and shake them in every direction to remind us that God surrounds us, we need all four of the items to make the blessing," she begins in her impeccable English accent. She sounds like the Queen. "It says in the Mishnah that the lulav—a frond from the date palm tree—has taste but no smell, symbolizing those who study Torah but do not possess good deeds. The hadass—myrtle—has a good smell but no taste, symbolizing those who possess good deeds but do not study Torah. The aravah—willow— has neither taste nor smell, symbolizing those who lack both Torah and good deeds. And of course, the etrog—the citron—has both a good taste and a good smell, symbolizing those who have both Torah and good deeds."

She pauses and looks around the table, her gaze resting on Honey, who, as dessert was being served, brought a plate of crumbly apple crisp to her father and then plopped herself down in Aaron's abandoned seat, right next to Naomi. Naomi gives her a warm smile. I shift in my seat, pulling my coat closer around me.

"Perhaps I am influenced by being a newlywed, but I cannot help but think that this is what makes a good marriage." Naomi Dayan turns to beam at her husband. He looks back adoringly. Miriam nudges me and mimes sticking her finger down her throat. I laugh despite myself. I turn to see Aunty Steph's reaction, but I'm not sure she's heard a word. She and Shmuel Yosef are having a silent conversation across the table, their eyes fixed on each other.

"We need friends and partners who complement us. Even if we think we have much to offer, or if we think we have nothing to offer. The etrog has both smell and taste—it has everything to offer—but you still cannot make the blessing on it alone."

I look at Honey sitting right next to Naomi Dayan. I look at Aunty Steph and Shmuel Yosef looking at each other. I swallow. Am I a willow with no smell and no taste—tied to the myrtle and palm, waved with the etrog—with nothing to offer beyond my presence?

＊　＊　＊

After lunch the next day, Aunty Steph and my mom are busy talking on the couch in the den. Max is at their feet wearing his space ranger costume, absorbed in an elaborate Lego Minifigure battle, and my dad is napping. Something tells me Honey won't be coming over today. So I head over to the Wines'.

When I get there, Miriam doesn't let us into the bathroom. "Are you making or just reading in there?" Honey demands. She rattles the doorknob.

"Honey and Shmuel Yosef sitting in a tree," Miriam sings from deep within.

Honey's ears turn red. "Go flush yourself down the toilet!" she yells through the door.

"K-I-S-S-I-N-G—"

We go to her room and flop on the floor.

"What do you think of Noam?" I ask her, trying to change the subject—sort of.

"I mean, honestly, anybody could tell you he's totally not suited for me," Honey says, ignoring my question and not noticing that my face flushed a bit when I asked it. "Shmuel Yosef is much more suited to your aunt. That was such a good idea to bring them together. Wasn't it?"

I guess it was *both* of our ideas that led to Aunty Steph and Shmuel Yosef meeting. I sigh when I remember him walking us home last night: When we got to the path between our streets, it wasn't wide enough for the three of us to go through together, so Aunty Steph waved me ahead while she and Shmuel Yosef followed behind, murmuring quietly in the darkness.

"Well, who knows what will happen," I say. "They haven't even been on one date yet."

"Puh-lease," Honey scoffs competitively. "Do I know my customers, or do I know my customers?" I peer at her and cock my head. I really don't get how Honey can move on from things so easily. When she stumbles, she just picks herself right back up.

"We might actually be really good at this," she cries. "We could start a business!" She leaps to her feet and gives a big stretch, almost like she's climbing out of clothes that are suddenly too small for her and leaving them in a pile on the floor.

"Hey, I have an idea," I say, the thought suddenly forming in my mind with perfect clarity. "How about we go shopping?"

"You mean by ourselves?"

I grin. "Yup. Just us."

"Definitely."

"No moms. Our choices."

"Yes."

"So," I say nonchalantly, "how about a vintage store?"

Honey's eyes open wide, and I know I've hit the jackpot. I flush with pleasure that she likes my idea. I might not be an etrog, but I'm not going to just sit back and be a willow either.

CHAPTER 8

WHAT GOES AROUND...
COMES AROUND

"Are you sure this is where your aunt gets her clothes?" Honey whispers to me.

"I didn't say this is where she comes specifically," I say a bit defensively. Nothing looks like the cool tunics and flowy skirts Aunty Steph wears. "But she says wearing vintage is not only cool but reduces your carbon footprint." We both nod knowingly.

I look at the racks of corduroy pants, wool skirts, and faded flannel shirts, the stacks of itchy-looking sweaters, the bins of shoes, and nod again. So does Honey. We are a few blocks from school at a second-hand clothing store called What Goes Around—by *ourselves.*

Honey fingers a pair of jeans with a red tag on the pocket.

"I thought your parents don't let you wear pants anymore?" I whisper.

"I'm just looking," she says. "Anyway, you're not allowed to wear pants out either."

"I am at camp," I say.

She raises her eyebrows. We both sigh.

"Ooh, try this," I say, pulling out a plaid button-down shirt from a rack. "And you can wear it with . . ." I pull out a mid-length jean skirt with buttons down the front. "This!" I say triumphantly.

Honey takes them from me and holds them up in front of her. "Plaid is really in," I say, smiling encouragingly. Honey doesn't have the best fashion sense. Also she wears a lot of hand-me-downs from her cousin Faigy so she's not used to choosing what she wants to buy. "And that skirt is super versatile. It'll match with so many things. Let's try it on."

We pull more things from the racks, and when our arms are full, we head to the changing room.

A saleslady cuts us off at the end of the aisle. "Can I help you?" she says, eyeing us suspiciously.

"We're fine, thanks," Honey says.

The saleslady purses her lips. "Girls, do your mothers know you're here?"

Honey and I look at each other. Technically our mothers—or fathers—don't. I bite my lip. Honey looks like she wants to shoot her hand to her hip, but her arms are draped with all the clothes.

"Our parents let us go shopping by ourselves," she says. "C'mon, Milla, let's go try on our things." She leads the way to the changing room. We squeeze in together, and Honey sweeps the curtain shut behind us with a flourish as we collapse into a fit of laughter.

Finally, we compose ourselves enough to try on the clothes, muffling yelps every time we jab each other with an elbow or bump butts.

"What do you think?" I strike a pose with my hands on my hips. "I know it's a sundress, but I could wear a T-shirt underneath."

"Um, Milla." Honey looks at me sideways as she struggles to get her arms into a stretchy velour dress. "I think it's actually an apron."

"Oh," I say. "Well, I could pin it and no one would notice."

I admire myself in the mirror. "Actually, it's perfect for Tammy Birnbaum's bat mitzvah this Saturday night—" I stop, quickly checking Honey's face. "Sorry," I say. Honey's not allowed to go because it's a dance party with boys at Tammy's house. My parents have said I can go if I don't dance with boys.

"Don't worry," she says, pulling the dress over her head. "It doesn't sound even remotely fun to me.

Anyway, remember—I'm going to sleep over at Tsippi Auerbach's that night with some friends from my old class."

"Great, so let's get you something to wear to that." I smile. "Plaid is very in."

"You said that already," she says from inside the velour dress, which now seems stuck on her head. She's wriggling all over the place, trying to get the dress on or off, I'm not sure anymore.

"Do you need help?" I ask her.

"No," she says, her arms raised and held tight above her head by the dress. She wiggles her shoulders to try and dislodge them, flails her bound arms, loses her balance, and falls over.

"Ooph!" I cry as she crashes into me on her way down and we come tumbling out of the changing room and land in a heap on the floor. My butt suddenly feels cold and exposed to the world.

I look at her on top of me, her head and shoulders stuck in the dress. I start giggling.

"What?" she says from inside the dress as I roll her off me. "Is there a problem?"

I accidentally let out a snort. Honey double-snorts back. We howl with laughter.

"Excuse me," I say, pinching my nostrils to imitate the saleslady's voice. "Excuse me, *girls*, but do your mothers know you're here?"

"Girls," a voice says sharply.

I look up—the saleslady is standing right over us.

Oh.

Um.

Oops.

My hand goes to my mouth before another snort can escape. The saleslady crosses her arms and taps her foot on the speckled carpet Honey and I are lying on.

"We're allowed to be here!" Honey says from inside her dress.

"Then behave like it," the saleslady snaps. I can't see Honey's face but mine sobers instantaneously.

I lead Honey back to the changing room and tug the dress off her. We try on the rest of our stuff, careful not to jab or even look at each other for more than a second in case we are tempted to start laughing again. Honey decides to get the red plaid shirt and jean skirt, and I get the sundress.

"It's off-putting to the other customers for you to use this establishment as your playground," the saleslady says tightly as she rings us up.

But when she hands me my purchase in a plain brown shopping bag, I clasp the handle firmly and feel emboldened.

"Thank you," I say. "Because, like your other customers, we believe that buying vintage is a great way to reduce your carbon footprint."

Honey elbows me in the ribs, and before the door has even finished jingling, we are laughing again, bumping into each other as we run down the street, our breath frosting and our navy plaid uniform skirts flapping against our knees.

An hour after Shabbat ends, I sail down the stairs, calling, "I'm ready!"

My parents drift into the front hallway from the kitchen, my dad holding his car keys.

"What on earth are you wearing?" my mother says.

"It's *vintage*," I say. "Like Aunty Steph wears."

My mom narrows her gaze in disapproval. "Did she give it to you?"

"Kind of," I lie.

"It looks like an apron."

"Well, I think it looks cool," I say, folding my arms in front of my chest.

"Our daughter is stating her need to begin eman-cipating herself from the influences and clutches of her parental units," my dad says.

"Jonathan!"

"What? I'm serious. Our little girl is growing up," my dad says.

"Trust me, I get it," my mom says.

"I think you look nice, Milla," Max says, sticking his head out from the den, where he's been watch-ing TV.

"Thank you, Max," I say, watching my mother's face as she deliberates if she's going to make me go upstairs and change. "Please, Mom?"

Her face softens, and she smiles ruefully. "I remember my first time going to a bat mitzvah." Then she shakes her head. "But I cannot let my daughter out of the house with safety pins running down her back. No way."

"Aunty Steph says you used to wear jeans with safety pins down the legs—on the *outside*," I say.

"That was considered the ultimate in cool, I'll have you know," she says. I raise my eyebrows. "Every-one did it," she adds defensively.

"Well, I'm not doing what everyone else does, I'm

being independent," I say, and I *know* I've got her. She and my dad share a private look.

"Thank you! Thank you!" I say, hugging her before she can change her mind.

"When the bat mitzvah party season gets in full swing, I'll take you shopping for some proper party dresses," she says, smiling. "And of course your own bat mitzvah dress."

Like all Tammy Birnbaum's birthday parties, her bat mitzvah party is in her basement. I mean, I guess it's not the same as a little-kid party with an entertainer—the basement is dark and pulsing with pop music—but it also doesn't feel like what I imagined a bat mitzvah would be like.

"Mazal Tov! I like your dress," I shout to Tammy over the din.

"Thanks, Milla, I like yours too."

"Thanks," I say. "It's vintage."

"Oh my god, Milla, I *love* your dress!" Tali squeals when I come over to stand with my friends. She's wearing a skirt and matching sweater—a Shabbat outfit.

"Me too!" Sophie says. She's also wearing a

Shabbat outfit along with her shul shoes. Sophie and Tali always agree before a party what they're going to wear, and then wear identically styled outfits. But looking around the room, it seems like no one was quite sure what is appropriate attire for our first class bat mitzvah. Ethan S. is wearing jeans and a T-shirt; Ethan W. is wearing a suit.

"It's cool," Natalie says. "But why do you have safety pins all down the back?" She's wearing a tight dress made out of stretchy material, with a soft pearl-gray fur vest on top.

"It's vintage," I say, enjoying the look on everyone's faces every time I say that. "Honey and me went to a thrift store—by ourselves." I pause for more looks of admiration.

"Yeah, too bad Honey couldn't come tonight," Natalie cuts in. She adjusts her vest and smooths her blown-out hair behind her shoulder. "Anyway, my mom took me to the mall for a shopping spree. She says we'll have so many parties coming up." It occurs to me that Natalie is wearing the perfect outfit for Tammy's bat mitzvah dance party. Also, my hand is itching to stroke the fur on her vest.

* * *

I had told my parents I wouldn't dance with boys, by which I meant that I would see when I got here. But it turns out Noam is sick and hasn't come. Anyway, the girls stand in one huddle and the boys in another and all we do is jump up and down. Tammy has a hopeful smile on her face, like at any minute someone might ask her to dance, but everyone stays in their huddles.

After a while, I go and stand by the drinks table with Tali and Sophie, who also aren't supposed to be dancing. I take the opportunity to drink a lot of soda, which my mother doesn't let me have. Then Tammy's dad, who is the DJ fiddling with his phone and a small speaker, puts on "Hava Nagila." The girls grab Tammy to do a hora with her, forming a circle and doing the grapevine step. At least we know how to do that one. The boys form a ring around us, pushing and pulling each other and being silly, whirling faster and faster until someone accidentally lets go and Ethan S. goes flying into a stack of folding chairs. Mrs. Birnbaum gives him ice and calls his mother.

Mr. Birnbaum puts on a song no one recognizes. I go back to the drinks table with Sophie and Tali, and Natalie joins us too.

"Can I be honest?" Natalie says. "Honey's not

missing anything. This party's a little lame." I kind of agree with Natalie's assessment, but I also feel indignant at her nerve. Natalie's bat mitzvah is in March, and she's already been regaling us with the details. Her dress, the chairs, the tablecloths: Everything will be matching black and gold. She is even in negotiation with her parents to change into a gold leotard and perform a routine with the dancers they've hired. I wish Honey *was* here to tell her off right now, and before I can stop myself, I just say what I imagine Honey would say.

"Not everyone can afford a fancy party," I tell Natalie pointedly.

Tali and Sophie exchange looks. Natalie just rolls her eyes.

"Chill out, Milla," she says. "I just meant it's not that fun. My mom says it's all about atmosphere—that that's the magic ingredient to any party and that no money can buy it. You either have it or you don't. You know what I mean?"

Natalie's mom is not someone I would ordinarily think of as wise, but she has a point here, not that I want to admit that right now. "How do you get it if you can't buy it?" I ask.

Natalie looks less certain suddenly. "She says it usually has to do with how much your friends like you." She shrugs.

"Not to speak loshon harah," Sophie says, which is always her and Tali's cue for when they are, in fact, about to say something negative about someone. "But I don't really understand this bat mitzvah party. There's nothing specifically Jewish here. Did she even do a mitzvah project?"

"Yeah," says Tali. "We've already started our tzedakah projects weeks ago." She gestures to Sophie and herself.

"Me too," Natalie says. "I'm raising money to buy pajamas for kids at a homeless shelter."

I look at all three of them in surprise. I haven't even thought of what I might do as a charity project, or started learning Megillat Rut with Aunty Steph. But Tali's and Sophie's bat mitzvahs are both in February, and Natalie's in March, so I guess that's only a few months away and they need to get ready. I still have plenty of time. I feel something bothering me on my back and reach behind to pull at my dress. I realize I've finished my third cup of Coke.

"I'm going to the bathroom," I say, breaking away.

When I get to the little door by the laundry room, it turns out Eitan Moses and Ethan W. have stuffed a roll of toilet paper into the toilet and flooded the bathroom. I give a wide berth as Mr. Birnbaum wades in with a plunger, but suddenly a slow song comes on and he changes his mind, discarding the plunger by the door and taking Mrs. Birnbaum by the hand. I shift from foot to foot, waiting for him to come back, but he and Mrs. Birnbaum sway like they are in their own world, their hips smushed together while the boys keep trying to "accidentally" push each other into them. Tammy stands off to the side by herself, her smile looking stuck to her face. Finally, after the third slow song, the lights go on, Mr. Birnbaum puts his phone back in his pocket, and the party's over. Everybody blinks at each other.

My dad texts me that he's waiting outside, and I say goodbye to Tammy, who is now sitting by herself on a folding chair, her skirt poofed up around her.

"Mazal Tov," I say again. "Thank you for the party."

"Bye, Milla. Thanks for coming. By the way, one

of your safety pins is open. You can see your tights. But I really like your dress, it's so cool. Where did you say you got it again?"

"It's vintage," I mumble, my face flaring as I hurriedly put my coat on.

The next day, I make Honey laugh when I tell her about the party and the Birnbaums and the toilet and about how I drank all that Coke and had to jiggle my leg in the car the whole way home.

"Anyway, don't worry, you didn't miss anything," I tell her.

"I wasn't worried," Honey says. She's wearing her new plaid shirt and jean skirt, the What Goes Around bag on the floor and the tags cut off and strewn about the carpet. "Everyone liked my outfit last night, by the way."

"Why don't we look in your closet and see what else looks good with your new shirt and skirt—I bet we can make lots of outfits," I say.

"I like it like this, the way you put it together," she says. Just then there's a loud knock and Miriam bursts in.

"Ima wants to know if you can peel potatoes and

then she wants you to watch Aaron because she has to take—" She stops when she sees the stuff on Honey's floor. There's a receipt poking out of the bag. Her eyes gleam.

"Did you go to What Goes Around?" she says. She must have very good vision because the bag is blank; only the receipt says the name of the store.

"And what if we did?" Honey says. "It's a thrift store. We are reducing our carbon footprint, for your information."

"Does Ima know?" Miriam crows, looking like she's just won the lottery. "Like, maybe I should tell her, for *her* information."

Honey and I look at each other. That Miriam, she really makes my blood boil.

"Ima won't care," Honey says defiantly. "Anyway, I paid for it with my own money."

"Wait, let me get this straight," Miriam says. "You kvetch about wearing our cousin Faigy's hand-me-downs—which are *free*—but you go and spend your own money to buy a stranger's old clothes?" She laughs, slapping her knee.

I guess Miriam has a point. But she's also missing something important.

"But we went ourselves," I interject. "We went *shopping*."

"I got to choose for myself," Honey says quietly. She's looking at her shirt and fingering the soft flannel. Miriam looks at it too.

"It is a cool outfit," Miriam admits after a moment.

"Thanks," Honey says. I can't help but notice that she doesn't mention I picked it out for her, or that it was my idea to go to What Goes Around.

"You know," Honey says to Miriam, "maybe when you're my age, you'll go shopping by yourself with a friend."

Miriam shrugs, and her face changes. "Go find Ima. She needs you," she says, and stalks out, slamming the door behind her.

When I get home, I take the apron out from the garbage bin under my desk, where I'd stuffed it last night. I smooth it out, refold it, and tuck it into the wicker basket that I keep my dolls' clothes in, deep in my closet. Then I sit back on my heels. Next time there's a bat mitzvah, I wouldn't mind going to the mall on a shopping spree with my mom too. But maybe I can use the fabric from the apron to make my dolls some outfits. And maybe I am mistaken, but was that a wistful look Miriam flashed at me and Honey before she slammed the door?

If it was, I have a suspicion that Miriam wasn't only thinking about shopping and choices—she was probably also thinking about friendship, and wishing she had one like mine and Honey's.

CHAPTER 9

BROTHERS

"Hi, Mom," I say, popping my head into Max's room. It is the last day of Chanukah and the first day of winter break, and she's on the floor in Max's room, laying out all his summer clothes, readying them to be packed. I am supposed to be packing too. We are going to Miami tomorrow to spend almost two weeks with my bubbie and uncles.

"Yeees?" my mom says, raising one eyebrow. She can tell I'm about to ask her for something.

"Can I go to Honey's, please? She just called—Mrs. Wine has to go out unexpectedly, and Honey asked if I can help her watch Aaron."

"Stay home by yourselves? *And* watch Aaron?" my mother says.

"What? Honey does it all the time," I say. Which is true. And it sounds like fun. I've never stayed home alone, never mind been in charge. "It'll be good experience," I tell my mother entreatingly. "Soon I can babysit for Max."

My mother blows air up into her bangs. "You said

you wanted to pack your clothes yourself this year."

"I'll pack as soon as I get back."

She exhales again, and I can practically see the wheels in her head turning, weighing "responsible" (packing for myself) with "responsible" (babysitting). I stand up straighter.

"As soon as you get back," she says, pointing her finger at me.

"As soon as I get back!" I promise, and smile my way out the door and over to the Wines'.

Mrs. Wine opens their front door with one hand, adjusting the wig sitting lopsided on her head with the other. As I enter, I see the black snood she covers her hair with when she's in the house flung on the banister.

"Hi, Milla, sweetie," she says breathlessly, then calling behind her: "Honey, you girls are in charge!" With that, she flies out the open door without a coat, jumps into the minivan, and speeds out of the driveway.

"Josh's in trouble again," Honey says, appearing from the kitchen and holding a mug. She's wearing the jean skirt and plaid shirt from What Goes Around. "The yeshiva just called. They've been threatening not to let him graduate, but it sounds like this time they're serious."

"Whoa," I say. "What did he do?"

"Something with Ari Schoenberg's tests." She shrugs. Then she grins. "But we have the house to ourselves. And Aaron. My bubbie took Miriam and Dan-Dan."

I grin back. Honey raises her mug to me. "I just made a pot of hot chocolate. You want some?"

"Sure," I say, following her to the kitchen.

"Hi, Aaron," I say, crouching down. He is sitting on the tiled floor under the oval kitchen table, humming the jingle from a cereal commercial and making piles out of small toy cars. "How you doing?"

"Aaron?" Honey prompts him.

"Hello," he says, focusing on balancing a car.

My father once explained to me that people can be autistic in different ways. He said it's a spectrum, and this means it's like there is a very long road that runs from downtown in the center of the city all the way to the countryside, and even though lots of people live on this road, they don't necessarily live anywhere near each other—or even in the same kind of house. He told me this after we were at a frozen yogurt place and a boy at the table next to us leaned over the booth and asked Max when his birthday was. When Max recited the month and date, and my mom supplied the year, the boy pronounced (correctly) that Max had been born on a Thursday.

"Phillip is our math guy," the boy's mom said, putting her arm around him.

Aaron is only six, but so far he's not a math guy. Or if he is, no one knows it.

"So this is what you have to do to make hot chocolate," Honey is saying now, carefully pouring it from the pot into a mug for me. I come over to where she is standing by the stove. "You make a paste out of cocoa and sugar with a bit of hot water. Then you boil the milk, but don't let it overflow. Then you add the paste to it and mix it really well so there're no lumps."

I take a sip. "It's delicious," I say, not for the first time wondering how Honey knows how to do this stuff. Also that her mother lets her. Does she have to negotiate for everything like I do? She was probably right that Mrs. Wine wouldn't have minded either way about us going shopping at What Goes Around. "Better than Starbucks," I add, and Honey laughs.

"Well, we're watching Aaron today anyway," she

says. She pours some hot chocolate into another mug. "Aaron, I'm letting yours cool off, okay?"

"Okay," he says, looking up at her for a moment.

I look through the bay windows at the Wines' snow-covered backyard and the park beyond their fence behind it. An early heavy snow fell last night. I think what it might be like to be an explorer and walk on places no one has ever walked before. Although now we know that most explorers weren't necessarily the first, they just were the first white men who thought they discovered places people had already inhabited for hundreds or thousands of years. But then there was Neil Armstrong, who walked on the moon the first time. I wonder if those explorers felt ordinary and insignificant when they were growing up too or if they always felt special.

"Do you think we'll ever be famous women because we've done something first?" I ask Honey. "Or even just something special—you know, make a mark in some way?"

"Definitely!" she says, hopping up on the counter with a big grin.

"Well, but—" I hesitate. I realize I asked the question wrong. I'm not worried if she will or not. Neither is she. "What about me? Do you really think I will?"

"If you want to." She shrugs. "I mean, why not?" I look at her. It sounds so simple, so reachable, the way she says it. She takes a sip of hot chocolate. "I hope Josh doesn't get expelled."

"What did he do with Ari Schoenberg's tests?" I ask. "I thought he graduated already."

"Yeah, Ari graduated," Honey says. "But he's, like, a Talmudic ace and he gave Josh all his old tests because everyone knows that Rabbi Bienenstock gives the exact same tests every year, so all Josh had to do was study from Ari's answers."

"Oh," I say. "Is that not allowed?"

"Well, it might have been fine if Josh had kept it quiet. But my brother is generous, and also an idiot: He photocopied the tests for all his friends. Using the school photocopier."

I laugh, and Honey does too. "Anyway, Ima says that if the rebbe was too lazy to make a new test and has been giving the exact same one for the last ten years, you can't get someone in trouble for studying off an old test." I nod and think how lucky the Wines are. Whenever I complain that something is unfair at school, my mother usually takes the teacher's side.

"Have you seen this one yet?" Honey says, sidling along the counter to open up a laptop. The laptop is brand-new—instead of each Wine kid getting a present for Chanukah, the laptop is a family gift and is to remain at the kitchen desk at all times. Although I like a lot of Mrs. Wine's ideas about how to treat kids, I think of all the gifts I got for Chanukah that are just for me, and I feel a little bad for Honey. But she seems to be truly excited about the laptop and is pulling up the latest of a string of Jewish-themed parodies to popular radio songs.

She jumps down, grabs a broom, and starts singing along, using it as a microphone. She points her finger at me, curls it toward herself to call me over, and hands me the dustbin for a duet. We play the song through a gazillion times, laughing more hysterically each time we bump our hips together with our dance moves. Just as I am about to hit the arrow for play again, Honey's eyes catch the full mug of hot chocolate cooling on the counter by the stove. She lets go of the broom.

"Where's Aaron?"

The wooden broom handle thumps on the floor. I look toward the oval table. Aaron and his piles are gone.

Still holding my dustbin, I slide toward the dining room and peer in. I don't hear anything. I crouch down under the dining room table: Some random Mr. Potato Head pieces and marbles litter the heavy carpet, but no Aaron.

"Aaron!" Honey calls. It's quiet.

We go into the den, but it's empty. The living room, laundry room, pantry, and bathroom are all empty too. Honey runs back to the front hall closet and starts swishing through the coats. She's pushing them to the side harder and harder. She jumps up and grabs hold of the shelf above the rack, scanning. Aaron can climb anything.

My heart drops into my stomach.

Aaron could be anywhere in the Wines' huge house. He's not very tall, and he likes to squeeze himself into small spaces. The extra fridges and freezers in the basement all have locks on them so that he can't crawl into one and accidentally get stuck inside. But there are a million nooks and crannies all over, in every room and every bathroom. And that is just inside.

Honey runs to the mudroom and unlocks the door that leads into the garage. "Aaron? Aaron?!" I lean around her to see. Bikes and scooters and pogo sticks and balls and sleds and hockey sticks are strewn everywhere. Folding tables and chairs are stacked precariously against the walls. Hoses snake across the grease-spotted floor. There is no room for a car to park here. And there's nowhere for a small six-year-old to hide either. My eyes land on the button for the automatic garage door opener.

"Do you think he could have opened the garage and gotten out?" I say.

"No!" Honey says, pushing me aside a bit. "It's closed, and he wouldn't have been able to reach the button by the door to do that."

"He *can* climb anything," I say. It wasn't such a stupid idea, was it?

She takes a breath. "Milla, you check all the other doors. Make sure they're all still locked. I'll start looking upstairs!" She flies up the winding main staircase two steps at a time, and I hear her banging the bedroom doors open. I run back to the living room and circle behind the couches, realizing suddenly that one of the glass cabinet doors is open. I hurry closer, registering a porcelain clockmaker on the carpet and that the lady with the balloons is missing. I have a glimmer of realization of what might have happened, but I don't stop to pick the clockmaker up. I tear through the dining room, the kitchen, and then the den. That's when I spot the stick that keeps the sliding door to the backyard in place. It is pulled up, and a draft of winter air blows in from a small crack where the door hasn't been slid shut all the way.

"Honey!" I shout. "Come quick!"

She is at my side in a second and the next second running out into the freezing day in her slippers.

"Aaron! AARON!" she shouts. Her voice pierces the thin air. "AARON, WHERE ARE YOU?" She runs across the lawn until she reaches the wooden fence that separates their yard from the park on the other side. The park is as big as several blocks, and the playground part is sheer across the other end, near shul. She looks up over the fence and pounds her fist against the wooden slats. "AARON?" she screams.

She runs to the wooden gate, but it's still latched. She looks at it, trying to determine if Aaron could have climbed the fence anyway, and that's when we hear it. A very faint humming. The cereal jingle.

"Aaron?" Honey shouts.

I realize there are light footprints in the snow,

different from Honey's frantic trampled route. And a trail of ruby-colored drips.

"Honey, there," I say, pointing up. Aaron is sitting on a branch of the big maple tree that is a fixture of the Wines' backyard and a nuisance to any game. The leaves are all fallen, and Aaron in his thin orange T-shirt stands out clearly against the gray sky. It looks like it is going to snow again. I see Aaron's toes curling against the branch and realize a second later that his feet are bare. He is grasping something in his hand.

"Aaron, come down!" Honey says, running toward the tree. She stops at the foot of it, and I see her take a deep breath. When she lets it out, it steams around her like she is in charge of making the clouds in the sky.

"Aaron," she calls gently now, hugging her arms around her body. "Aaron."

I stand frozen in place. I don't know what to do. I stare at the drips of blood on the white snow.

"Milla, go get our coats," Honey commands, turning to me for a second before she looks back up again. I run to the mudroom and pull off the first two things I find and everything else on that hook falls to the ceramic floor with a thump. I stuff my feet into someone's boots and grab two more. When I run back out with all the stuff falling out of my arms, Honey is still standing at the bottom of the tree in her slippers, speaking quietly up to Aaron. As I approach with the coats and boots, I think I hear her saying, "It's okay, Aaron, you're not in trouble," but she waves me back and continues to talk in a soft voice.

Then Aaron nods his head up and down.

"Hot chocolate?" he says. "Okay." He nods one more time and climbs down, lightly tapping Honey's outstretched hand with his own in their fist bump. Honey tries to give him a piggyback to the house, but after a few steps, he squirms away and skips in his bare feet through the shallow snow ahead of us. All our trampling and footprints have marked up the backyard so that it looks like a Chutes and Ladders board.

Honey expertly bandages Aaron's finger, wraps him tightly in the big blanket from the den, and gently pushes him onto the couch. He is shivering. She sits next to him, holding him close.

"Milla, the hot chocolate!" she says. "Heat it up."

"Um." I grimace and shift my feet. "I don't know how to turn on the stove."

"Just stick the mug in the microwave, Milla."

I've never used the Wines' microwave before, but her tone makes me feel foolish, so I just turn into the kitchen, shove the mug into the microwave, and press some buttons. It starts. When it beeps that it's done, I open it back up: Half the hot chocolate has overflowed over the side and onto the tray. I grab a paper towel and mop up as best as I can and carry the mug carefully into the den.

Honey has taken the broken old lady, severed from her balloons, and placed both pieces on the coffee table. "It's okay, Aaron," she repeats over and over again, tears trailing silently down her cheeks as she rubs his arms under the blanket. I bring the hot chocolate, and Honey takes it from me, holding it gently to Aaron's lips.

Aaron's face looks the same as it always does: like a cute six-year-old boy's, framed by the same golden hair as Honey's, with the same smattering of freckles across his nose and cheeks but without any clue—at least to me—what he might be feeling. I swallow when I think about how I avoid looking at Max's face whenever I leave for Honey's on Shabbat afternoons. I don't want to see him looking sad. Does Aaron know he was in danger—and that it was our fault? Does he know how scared we were, and had he been scared too? Can he feel how much Honey loves him? My dad says that studying Talmud is like being a lawyer: It is about learning rules, understanding them, and then applying them to situations. But people are not like that, and what other people think or feel—or what I might think and feel—is only a starting point, a jab in the dark about what someone else might be thinking or feeling. With people, there is no Ari Schoenberg who knows all the answers, and there is no Josh Wine to make sure everybody else knows them too.

The front door bangs closed. "I'm back!" Mrs. Wine calls.

"Are you going to tell her?" I whisper to Honey. She wipes her cheeks and nose and nods.

"Honey? Aaron?" Mrs. Wine calls.

"In here, Ima."

Mrs. Wine enters the den through the kitchen, her hands on her head as she's putting on the snood. I see her register Aaron wrapped in a blanket, Honey with tear tracks on her cheeks, and the broken balloon lady on the coffee table. She drops her hands, and without saying a word, she comes over and eases herself onto the couch, Honey scooching over a bit so she can squeeze in.

"Oh, Aaron," she says in an exhale, and closes her eyes for a minute when Honey quickly gives her the gist of what happened.

I am perched on the edge of a recliner, and I try not to stare at Mrs. Wine's hair. It is short, almost just stubble in the back, and completely gray. Her face, always pink whether underneath a dark blond sheitel or the black snood, and animated—joking with one of the boys, concerned over a story Susie is telling her, showing Honey how to do something—is gray and still.

"I'm sorry, Ima," Honey says in a small voice. "I'll be more careful next time."

Mrs. Wine pushes the snood to her forehead and down to the nape of her neck, and her face comes to life again. "We will just be thankful to Hashem that we are sitting here now together," she says. Honey leans into her, and Mrs. Wine puts her arm around her, guiding Honey's head onto her shoulder, her other hand lightly rubbing Aaron's back. It is quiet except for Aaron's soft humming. I stare at the broken pieces of the old lady with the balloons and wonder if I should leave.

Then Mrs. Wine smiles at me, and her eyes light on the broken balloon. "Stuff is . . . really just stuff," she sighs, like we are continuing a conversation we've had before. "But I suppose our stuff makes us who we are." She moves her arm from around Honey to scratch underneath her snood for a minute before replacing it and giving Honey a squeeze.

"Those china figurines were my grandmother's," Mrs. Wine says after a moment. "I've loved this old lady with the balloons since I was a little girl and would play with her whenever I came here to my grandmother's house. Even though we are supposed to be as tznius as we can in all ways—to be modest in our dress and our actions, to need little, to be humble—it is still important to have dignity and to have identity."

I wonder if Miriam told Mrs. Wine about the shopping after all. Or if Honey did. I look at Mrs. Wine in her long black skirt, white shirt, and long black cardigan. She wears the same style outfit every day, like a uniform. She sighs again and looks at Honey. "But, girls, baruch Hashem, most important is that we are thankful for what we have." Then she turns her gaze to me and smiles. "And that includes good friends." I smile back and try to catch Honey's eye, but her head is still on Mrs. Wine's shoulder and her eyes are closed, her fingers idly picking at a small spot on her skirt where the denim has frayed.

"I'm back!" I call when I get home.

"In here!" my mother calls. I find her in her room surrounded by orderly piles of her own summer ward-robe, an open suitcase on her bed. "How did it go?" she asks.

I ignore her question. "Don't worry, I'm going to pack now," I tell her.

"It's fine, Milla," she says. "I already did it for you."

"What? Why?" I protest. "I said I would do it myself."

"Well, I didn't know when you'd be home, and I wanted it done and done." She swipes her hands each time she says "done." "And done neatly. So just say thank you."

"Oh," I say. "Thanks. I guess." I look out the win-dow. It was still light just a few minutes ago when I was walking home, but the winter day is already turn-ing to a dark blue dusk.

My mother has turned her attention back to packing. "I'll go find Max," I say.

"He's in his bedroom," my mother says without looking up from the blouse she is crisply refolding.

I find Max lying on his bed on his stomach playing a video game, his tablet glowing in the dark. I turn on his light for him, and he glances over his shoulder, his face lighting up when he sees it's me. Or what I can see of it anyway. He is wearing the blue-and-yellow coveralls of a movie character, complete with yellow bathing cap and goggles.

"Hey, Max. No space ranger today?"

"In the wash," he says. "Mom said he needed to be clean or we couldn't take him to Florida." I notice his small suitcase open against the dresser, his clothes neatly folded inside.

"Good idea," I say with a smile. It occurs to me that, like Mrs. Wine, Max also has a uniform. And Max even likes to keep his head covered too. I laugh when I think of my comparison.

"What's so funny?" Max says.

"Nothing," I say, still smiling. "Want me to help you build your new Lego?"

He springs off his bed. "Really, Milla? Sure! Daddy

said it'll have to wait until we get back from Miami because he doesn't have time, but we could do it together now!" He's dragging me over to the little table in his room and holding the instructions booklet out to me before I can blink. "Look!"

I sit down on one of the low red wooden chairs at the table where the Lego airplane my parents got him for Chanukah is all laid out in closed bags, waiting for someone to help him get started. I turn the instruction booklet to page one.

"Okay, let's get scissors and open the first bag."

"It's going to be so cool! Right, Milla?" he says, fetching blue plastic kid's scissors from his desk.

"You bet," I say. "Maybe when it's done, my dolls can go on a plane ride." I reach out and adjust his goggles, pushing them on top of his yellow-bathing-capped head. Whatever his costume—or uniform—it's always nice to see my brother's face.

I guess I might not show it enough, but I hope Max knows how much I love him too.

Mitzvah

CHAPTER 10

CONTROL

On the plane to Miami, I read a book called *Cashews* by Sylvia Lim that Mr. Sandler assigned us to read over winter break. It's part of our unit on heroes in literature, but so far the main character, Nathan Almond, seems anything but: He's a boy with a nut allergy and very bad luck who is forced to work in a nut factory. But I am looking forward to spending time with my favorite heroine, Daisy, when I reread all six Most Likely To . . . books over break.

When we get to Miami, it is warm and sticky. As we wait in line at the airport rental car agency, I peel off my hoodie and breathe in the familiar air. Lots of my friends go to Florida for winter break, but for me this is more than a vacation. I think of it like one of those friendship lockets that say BEST FRIENDS. Instead of two halves, my locket would be divided into a whole bunch of pieces that say BEST FAMILY, with one of the biggest pieces right here in Miami.

My bubbie meets us at the apartment we always rent in her condo complex. As usual, she greets us with big hugs and a plateful of her sugar cookies.

"Milla, just look at you!" she says, holding my face in her hands. "Almost a bat mitzvah girl."

"Almost," I say. While my parents unpack, I look at myself in the hallway mirror, wondering if my bubbie really sees something different in me, or if she is just saying that because she's my grandmother. I peer closely: To me, I look the same.

After we've had a swim, we go to Uncle Dougie and Auntie Jacqui's house for dinner. My almost-two-year-old twin cousins toddle out stark naked. Auntie Jacqui explains that she's toilet-training them.

"Say hi to Milla and Max," she tells them.

"Hi, Mi-ya. Hi, Max," Ollie says.

"Hi, Mi-ya. Hi, Max," Oskie says too.

"It's Mi-LLa," Max coaches them.

"I don't mind," I say, bending down to give them hugs. "Mi-ya can be your special name for me, right, guys?"

"Right, Mi-ya!" they shout together. I laugh and pretend to chase them. Soon Uncle Dougie comes home, and then Uncle Robbie arrives with pizza. We are sitting at the large round patio table in the back-yard when Ollie and Oskie toddle over to us together, saying, "Osh it, osh it." They are holding matching toy dump trucks covered in mud and sand, which they promptly set on the grass—and pee on.

"All clean now," Oskie says, holding up his truck for us to see.

"All keen," Ollie agrees, showing us his truck too.

"Oh dear," my mother says, backing away with a horrified look on her face while Max and I burst out laughing. "Jacqui, you know the parenting experts suggest two and a *quarter* years old as the optimum time for toilet training. That's what I did with my kids. Not to step on your toes, but I'm not sure these two are *quite* ready."

"They seem to know what they're doing just fine to me," my dad says with a chuckle. "Their control—and aim—is remarkable."

Auntie Jacqui just laughs her big laugh and grabs the green garden hose, spraying down Ollie, Oskie, and their trucks.

Soon we settle into a rhythm. I swim with Max in the ocean and the pool while my mom emails about board chairperson stuff from a deck chair and my dad fields work calls from under an umbrella. I play gin rummy for nickels with my bubbie. Uncle Robbie stops by most mornings with coffee for my parents and Bubbie and teaches me to play backgammon. In the afternoons, we go to Uncle Dougie and Auntie Jacqui's house and play with Ollie and Oskie. "Osh it!" Max and I have been saying and laughing every time we need to *wash* something. Or splash each other in the pool. It's our inside joke.

On Friday night, we have Shabbat dinner all together at my bubbie's condo. Everyone is laughing and talking over each other, in a way that reminds me of being at the Wines'. I wish Aunty Steph could be with us too, but it's still fun to be with so many pieces of my locket for once.

"Your mother." Uncle Robbie shakes his head to me, still laughing at Uncle Dougie's dead-on imitation of my mother's expression when something has not gone to plan. "It was always her way or the highway."

"It still is," I say, and everyone laughs, even though I'm not sure I really meant it to be funny.

On the last day, it rains, and my mother leaves Max with Auntie Jacqui and my bubbie and takes me to a big department store to shop for bat mitzvah dresses.

Music plays in the background, and the air smells of perfume. My mother goes straight over to a rack of dresses and starts pulling things off and putting them over her arm. I go to a different rack and browse. I don't know what I'm hoping to find, but I think I'll know it when I see it.

"What do you think of this?" I say, holding up a navy tulle dress that could be good for one of my friends' parties.

My mother screws up her face. "It's okay. I guess you could try it on and see. What about this?" She shows me a dark floral outfit with an oversized collar.

"It's nice, but it's not my style."

My mother rolls her eyes and drapes the outfit on top of the others on her arm anyway. "Just try it on. You never know."

"This?" I say, holding up a dress with gold embroidery.

She shakes her head. "That material looks chintzy."

"It looks nice to me," I say, putting it back on the rack. She's right, several of the threads are already loose.

She holds up something light and silky in peach.

"Oh my goodness, what about this for *your* bat mitzvah? It will look so good with your coloring."

"It's pretty," I say, cocking my head.

"Ladies, can I help you?" A sales assistant appears beside us. "Let me take these from you and start a fitting room. You just carry on browsing, and when you're ready, let me know." He takes the piles from me and my mother and disappears. My mom and I make our way through the racks. Finally, our arms laden with more items, we head to the fitting room area. The sales assistant opens up a big corner room for us with mirrors all around and our chosen outfits hanging from rails along one of the walls. He takes what's in our arms and adeptly adds them to the rails. My mother sinks into a chair in the corner.

I try everything on. Some things are nice; some things are terrible. Some things we put in a "maybe" pile. After an hour, I am exhausted. I open my water bottle and sit cross-legged on the carpet looking at myself in triplicate.

"Okay, let's make some decisions," my mother says, standing up. She goes to the "yes" pile and starts holding things up. "This one for Tali's; this one for Sophie's. This one for Natalie's. And this one for yours. You don't need one for Rivkie—or Honey—because they're not having parties; you can just wear a shul outfit, which you have plenty of."

I look up at my mother through our reflections in the mirrors. "Mom, I'm not sure I need this many dresses."

"Well, of course you don't need something different for every bat mitzvah, but this should get you started." She holds the peach one up against herself and smiles at her reflection.

I stand up and take the dress from her, holding it against myself. In the mirror, side by side, I realize that I am only two or three inches shorter than her. "I do like it, but I'd rather wear it to Natalie's—I can even wear it to Sophie's and Tali's too—and get something else for my own bat mitzvah."

"Something else? Like what?" She gestures to the rails covered in the dresses I've tried on.

"I don't know." I bite my lip. "Mom, it's just not what I had in mind."

"Well, what *did* you have in mind?"

"I don't know. Just not this."

She's wearing the expression Uncle Dougie was imitating.

"Well, this is a beautiful dress," she says. "Not to mention expensive. It looks perfect on you. What more could you want?"

"It looks perfect to you but not to me," I mumble, feeling miserable.

"Milla Ruth, what does that mean?" she says, but I stop answering because I'm afraid I'm going to cry.

When we pay, I try not to appear ungrateful. We got some really pretty things. It adds up to a lot of money.

"What a lucky girl," the sales assistant says with a smile as he carefully folds the dresses and puts them in two large shopping bags.

"I know," I say quietly.

"Trust me, Milla," my mom says as we step into the muggy parking lot and wait for my dad to pick us up. It has stopped raining, but the air feels heavy and pregnant, like any minute the skies will open to a downpour. "That dress is *the one*. Just say thank you."

"Thank you," I say, keeping my gaze on a puddle, the plastic shopping bag handles slippery in my fingers.

The first day back at school, I feel blah—gray skies, mottled slush frozen over the street curbs, and the zipper of my ski jacket gets caught on my uniform sweater. When I tug it loose, my sweater tears. Then there's a substitute for English. She writes *Ms. Silver* on the whiteboard.

"Right, okay, guys, so what are the themes in *Cashews*?" she says, jumping right in. I know the answer, but I'm not raising my hand until I see how things go.

"Anyone?"

No answer.

"Did anyone read this book?" Ms. Silver says.

I'm pretty certain that we have all read it. Mr. Sandler asked us to.

"Well, okay, we'll just start from scratch," Ms. Silver says. She sits on the desk, crosses one leg over the other, and opens a well-worn copy of the book.

Who is this person? She isn't acting like she's a substitute. She's acting like she thinks she's our teacher. Where is Mr. Sandler?

Later that night, I overhear my parents talking in the kitchen.

"It became a standoff," my mother says. "Raphael

Sandler said he'd had it and told Rabbi Adler he quit. Luckily Sue Eisen's sister-in-law was in-between things and agreed to fill in at the last minute."

"A standoff about what?" my father says.

"Apparently they've been butting heads since Rabbi Adler came. But the final straw was that Mrs. Benzaquen is retiring at the end of this year and Rabbi Adler wants to start a formal search for the new head of English—and have Raphi interview for the position like anyone else, rather than just promoting him."

"I thought everyone loves him. Milla certainly thinks he's a great teacher."

"They do, but we brought Adler in to be an administrator and he feels likes this is the way to do things properly, even if they'll ultimately give the job to Raphi. But Raphi said forget it and that he doesn't need this job."

"What does that mean?" my dad says. "I thought he has little kids to support."

"I don't know," my mom says. "I mean, he would get hired in a second by any of the other schools. I've heard Kedem School is frothing for him. But honestly, I never understood why he went into teaching.

He had such a promising career. He was totally on the partner track at Lowell Minkoff."

I hug my knees in my fuzzy pajama pants as I sit at the top of the stairs. I didn't know Mr. Sandler used to be a lawyer. Or that he has little kids. Or that his name is Raphael. *Raphi.* And aren't adults always telling us to get along, to find a way to work things out?

"You left your partner-track job," my dad says.

"That's different. Max needed me. I needed to be home for my family."

"We would have been fine if you kept working too, honey. We would have made it work. It was a choice you made."

"It didn't feel like a choice," my mother says flatly.

"That doesn't mean you can't change things now," my dad says.

She must be filling the kettle because their voices get lost first in the rush of water from the tap and then in the heavy whoosh of boiling water. I hug my knees tighter. This doesn't sound like their usual bantering. My mother sounds upset.

The whooshing stops, and I can hear my parents' voices again.

"Well, they didn't even bring it to the board or we

never would have let it get to this point," my mom says. She pauses. "But the board needs to support Adler, of course."

"Lori," my dad says.

"I know," she says heavily. "I feel sick about the whole thing."

"Can you make it right?"

There's a pause. "I'll try," she says.

Mr. Sandler taught us that while the plot of a story is what happens in it, the theme is the main idea that you can take away and think about afterward. I didn't raise my hand in Ms. Silver's class, but if I had, I might have said that the theme in *Cashews* is what happens when someone is unfairly punished, and whether some people are just lucky or unlucky, or whether we all have control over our own fate and destiny. I feel it's unlucky Mr. Sandler got in a fight with Rabbi Adler, and I am not sure if this was his fault and whether it was something he could have controlled or not. It's unlucky for our class, and for me, that we aren't going to have Mr. Sandler anymore.

"Mr. Sandler stood up for what he believed in, and for *himself*—that has nothing to do with lucky or unlucky," Honey says the next day after school. She's on the massage table in our extra room, her ponytail loosened and pushed back so she can lie flat, staring up at the ceiling. There were all kinds of rumors flying around in the hallways at school about where Mr. Sandler is and if Ms. Silver is here to stay, but I didn't tell anyone except Honey what I overheard from my parents.

"Yeah, but was it his *destiny* to get in a fight with Rabbi Adler or could he have avoided it?" I say.

"Milla, what does it matter? It's like you're asking about hashgachah pratis."

"What's that?"

"It's like you're asking if Hashem *makes* people do things or if we have free will to decide things for ourselves."

"Oh," I say. I guess she's right.

"Milla, all we know is what happened, happened. They both made choices."

"Yeah. It's just . . . He acted like we were really important to him, like he really cared about us," I say. "But then he just left us."

Honey looks at me funny. "Don't you think you're being a little mean?" She doesn't say "selfish," but I'm pretty sure that's what she's implying. I square my jaw and don't say anything. She's facing the ceiling again. "All we can do is control the things we can control. I've been thinking about that for myself..."

I wait to hear what she is going to say, but she just stares at the ceiling. I think about Daisy in my Most Likely To . . . books. Her parents felt they had no control over their lives when they were part of their Hasidic community. They think they're giving Daisy something better—the freedom to choose her clothes, her friends, her studies, her life. To be friends with who she wants, learn what she wants, and be whoever she wants to be. But she doesn't appreciate it because even though there's endless opportunity for her, she doesn't have things that could anchor her—like grandparents and cousins and knowing where you come from. And she feels like she *doesn't* know who she is. Because certain choices have been taken away from her.

I shake my head in confusion. Maybe choices make us who we are? I look at Honey, who's lapsed into silence on the massage table. I think about Mrs. Wine and her uniform and the porcelain lady with the balloons and wonder if she meant that we use our stuff and our clothing—which are on the outside—as a way of expressing who we are on the inside. But sometimes the outside doesn't match the inside.

I look at my mother's bat mitzvah portrait, leaning against the wall by the massage table. How could I have forgotten: Her dress is peach. I roll my eyes and then sigh to myself. Is *my* bat mitzvah dress my mother's way of expressing that I should be just like her?

"Honey?" I say.

"Hmm?" she says.

"Were you going to tell me something?"

"Never mind," she says.

"Okay, then, can I take a turn?" I say, nudging her off the massage board and climbing up to do more thinking.

On Monday, Mr. Sandler strides into class like nothing ever happened. He writes *mea culpa* on the whiteboard and waits for us to settle down.

"Kids, mea culpa. That's Latin for 'my bad.' I made a mistake. I made a bad choice. I felt at a crossroads in my life, and I let my own ego get in the way of one of my missions in life—teaching young minds and preparing them to be critical thinkers. And some other stuff they tell me to teach. Can you forgive me?" He looks out at us.

I nod my head vigorously. It's a relief to have him back. Of course I forgive him. Everyone around me is nodding too and smiling.

"Thank you," he says. He waits a moment to make sure we know that he really means it.

"Are you back for good?" Natalie asks.

"Well, I'm back for now—and in this life, maybe that's as much as we can ever know." He raises his eyes to the ceiling, and even though his grin is playful, I think he means that God is in charge of the rest. Or maybe just what Honey said on the massage table: Some things aren't in our hands, so all we can do is control what we can.

"All right, who can tell me the theme of *Cashews*?" All the hands in the class shoot up. "Milla, go for it."

"It's like in my favorite book, *Most Likely To... Daisy*," I say. "It's all about choices and the extent to which you can control your life."

Mr. Sandler clears his throat, and I catch a funny expression cross his face. "I am familiar with that series, Milla," Mr. Sandler says. "But I was asking about *Cashews*."

"Oh, right." I blush. "Well, um, I guess you could say it's about a boy who feels ordinary, but also, um, *extraordinary*. It's also about something he can't control, which is being unlucky. And how he changes his destiny."

"Interesting interpretation, Milla," Mr. Sandler says, looking closely at me. "But I like it."

A little light turns on inside my heart, and when its beam comes out through my smile, I don't try to hold it in. I'm so happy Mr. Sandler is back.

CHAPTER 11

BAT MITZVAH SEASON

I'm still thinking about external and internal choices as the bulletin board above my mother's computer station in the kitchen fills up with invitations: bright ones, pastel ones, shiny ones, and glossy ones.

Rivkie Feuerstein's father is a rabbi, and for her bat mitzvah, her parents sponsor a kiddush in their shul the second Shabbat after we come back from winter break. Since none of us live near Rivkie, her mother invites all the girls in our class to sleep over. On Friday night, we sit at long folding tables in her living room eating steaming bowls of neon yellow chicken soup, dry roasted chicken, maroon meatballs, and potato kugel. Rivkie doesn't say a word throughout the whole meal, but her dad leads us in singing Shabbat songs that we belt out at the top of our lungs. It's like being at camp. We sleep in sleeping bags on the floor of her basement, and the next day, we all go to shul bleary-eyed, earlier than I've ever had to go before—because Rivkie's dad is the *rabbi*!

"Aren't you going to eat something?" I ask Honey at the kiddush, finding her sitting on a chair against a wall by herself. I've loaded up my plate with potato kugel, herring, cholent bean stew, chips, and my favorite, eire kichel cookies with big crystals of sugar sprinkled on top.

"You can share with me," I say, passing her my fork and nudging her over so I can share her chair.

"I'm fine," she says, pushing the fork back to me.

"Suit yourself," I say, digging in to the hot potato kugel. It's not like Honey not to elbow her way in for kiddush food, never mind not eat, and I know something's up—but there's no use pressing when she's quiet like this.

Afterward, we go back to Rivkie's house, where her mother has set up a buffet lunch: cold deli meat, cucumber salad, and more potato kugel, plus a birthday cake for dessert. Then Rivkie stands up and gives a dvar Torah. Everyone listens quietly while she speaks just above a whisper. When she is done, she says, "Good Shabbos, thank you for coming to my bat mitzvah." Her cheeks are pink and her eyes sparkle, like she had been sleeping all this time and suddenly woke up to a party that was for her. Is that how I'll feel in June?

"How was it?" my mother asks when she picks up Honey and me after Shabbat ends Saturday night. Honey is still quiet.

"Fine," I say.

"Just fine?" she says. "Can I get a little more information?"

"Mom," I groan. "It was nice, it was good, what else do you want to know?"

"Honey, how was it?" my mom says.

"Well, Lori, to be honest, I don't think it was what either Milla or I would have wanted for ourselves, but Rivkie was really happy and it seemed like it was exactly the right bat mitzvah for her."

I shoot Honey a look: suck-up!

"Thank you, Honey, that's a lovely grown-up answer," my mother says. I stick my tongue out at Honey.

I wait for her to stick hers out back, but she keeps her face forward. "You're welcome."

It's not until after we drop her off that I remember Honey's bat mitzvah is in a few weeks. Her parents have planned a kiddush in shul on Shabbat. Is that why she was so quiet all day?

The next Thursday night is Tali's bat mitzvah and then on Sunday night it's Sophie's.

"Girls, did you have fun?" Mrs. Wine asks me and Honey as we walk to her car after Sophie's. Mrs. Wine was there too, and her face is still flushed pink from all the Jewish dancing.

"Yes, Ima," Honey says quietly, even though she hardly got up to dance the whole night.

"Yeah, it was fun," I say.

"Well, I enjoyed myself too. Baruch Hashem, it was a lovely simcha," Mrs. Wine says. She swings herself up into the driver's seat of her minivan, closes the door, and bends down to pull off her high heels.

"Sophie and Tali are best friends, and they did the *exact* same party. Why didn't they just share it?" I muse as Mrs. Wine is putting on her winter boots. At each of their bat mitzvahs, Sophie and Tali wore frilly dresses, had arts and crafts activities for us to do for charity, spoke about doing charity in their speeches, did the best friend's speech for the other, and had the same music and dances.

Before I can say that they were both fun despite being so similar, Honey snaps, "They're best friends, Milla, not *sisters*."

"No, I know—I was just—joking," I say, stung, and then annoyed because she still hasn't told me what's making her so crabby lately.

"A bat mitzvah is such a special milestone for a girl's whole family," Mrs. Wine says. "Even if it's something small, it's a wonderful way to celebrate their daughter as an individual, and to welcome her entry to being a bas Torah and accepting the laws of Judaism for herself."

"Ima, can you start the car already? It's freezing!"

I raise my eyebrows in surprise at Honey's tone. Mrs. Wine is not an eyebrow raiser, but I think I see them creep up as she turns her head and gives Honey a look. Then she gives her boot a final tug, swings her legs back to the pedals, and starts the minivan. I rest my head against the cold window, suddenly bone-tired and looking forward to putting on my pajamas.

A few weeks later, an expected glittering black-and-gold invitation shaped like a mask arrives in the mail. Gold sparkled curlicued letters spell out *superstar* and *hot stuff* and, of course, *NATALIE*. We are supposed to come wearing our fanciest outfits.

"Ask your parents again," I tell Honey. We are sitting with our legs dangling from the counter in the Wine girls' bathroom.

"They're just going to say no," Honey says, beating her heels in a rhythm against the cabinet under the sink. "Abba and Ima say it's going to be 'inappropriate' and they don't feel it 'aligns with our family's religious observance and values'—or something like that."

I look at Honey sympathetically. I don't exactly know what the Wines mean by "inappropriate," but I think it has to do with the fact that when Micah went to Natalie's older brother Effie's bar mitzvah last year, he came home telling stories about the dancers in bikini tops. And that there were people kissing in the bathroom. And that Itzie Lieb got drunk. Honey's parents didn't even want her at Tammy's party, so I guess if Effie's bar mitzvah is anything to go by, Natalie's might not be "appropriate." But still, I wonder why it was okay for *Micah* to go to Effie's bar mitzvah to begin with. At the very least they knew there would be disco-type dancing.

"But anyway, I don't care," Honey says non-chalantly.

I look at her in disbelief. She doesn't care that her parents aren't letting her go to Natalie's bat mitzvah? Natalie *Aronovich's* bat mitzvah?

"But Natalie's been saying she'll probably ask you, me, Sophie, and Tali to do her best friend's speech," I say. I've already been planning what we could write for it, maybe do a funny song. None of us actually feel like we're *best* friends with Natalie, but we're still a group.

Honey looks at me like I'm one of her brothers—who has just passed some massively stinky gas. "I said I don't *care*, Milla. I've got more important things to think about."

"Like what?" I say.

She hops off the counter and turns to look at me. "Okay. What do you think about me leining?"

I look at her like she has just asked me what I think about her asking her parents if she can get a pet lion.

"Like, your bat mitzvah...parsha?" I say incredulously.

I think Honey might have just indicated that she wants to chant the portion of the Torah read in shul the Shabbat closest to her turning twelve. Or rather, if she was a boy, the portion that the bar mitzvah boy would read when he was called up to the bima to make a blessing on the Torah for the first time. And, while I do know that for Reform and Conservative Jewish girls it is totally common for them to have bat mitzvahs and do all this leining and blessings, in our Orthodox world it is pretty much unheard of and logistically impossible.

Without even getting into the specifics of the Jewish laws, which I don't really know, once we turn bat mitzvah, we can't go into the men's section anymore—where the bima is—so where would a girl read the Torah from?

"Wait," I whisper, my eyes wide. "In a partnership minyan?" As far as I can tell, people like Honey's family would just as soon go to a Reform temple than be caught dead in a partnership-style service, which still have separate men and women's sections but give women more opportunity to lead the prayers.

"I was thinking about Megillas Esther," Honey says calmly. "At a women's-only service."

"Oh," I say, feeling my mouth make a small circle.

"I *was* born on Purim."

"You were," I say, considering this. Megillat Esther is the story of the exceptionally brave Queen Esther, who with her uncle Mordechai risked her life to save the Jewish people from the evil Haman, who wanted to destroy them. Does Honey feel a connection to Esther other than being born on the holiday where the megillah is read twice? She's never had to risk her life like Esther, but she is definitely someone I consider brave.

"I thought your parents were making a kiddush the Shabbos after Purim. I thought that's all you wanted," I say instead.

"I don't care about a kiddush either way. And I don't want a party. But I do want to *do* something," Honey says.

"But I'm *doing* something," I say. "I've just started learning Megillat Rut with Aunty Steph—why don't you learn Megillat Ester and give a dvar Torah?"

"I knew Micah's whole bar mitzvah parsha better than him, just from listening to him practice," Honey says, ignoring my point. "And I knew Josh's and Ezra's too."

"Okay, but, Honey, Purim is in a month," I say practically. "Don't guys spend, like, a year learning for their bar mitzvah?"

"I could just do a chapter," she says. "I don't have to do the whole thing."

"But who's going to teach you? And who's going to come? And what—" I don't know why, but I feel overwhelmed by a long list of objections as to why this isn't going to work out for her.

"Thanks for the support, Milla," Honey snorts.

"No, it's just—"

I suddenly realize she's been thinking about this a long time. This is what's been bothering her. But now she's figured out what she wants to do about it. Her chest is pulled up tall and straight, and her hands are on her hips like Wonder Woman. Then she shrugs.

"I think I can do it," she says simply, and hops back up next to me on the bathroom counter. "And I called Naomi Dayan—she says if my parents say okay she'll teach me."

"Well, great," I say, knowing that my enthusiasm sounds fake. But what I don't know is why can't I make it sound—or feel—genuine?

A week later, I catch Honey humming the special tune for chanting the megillah while she is doing dishes from Shabbat lunch.

"Wait, your parents said yes?" I say.

"Yup," she says without turning around.

"Wow," I say, swallowing. I am sitting at the island munching potato chips. "Naomi's started teaching you already?"

"Yup."

"How's it going?" I ask.

"Good," she says.

"Do you know the whole thing already?"

"Hmm," she says noncommittally.

"I still can't believe your parents said yes."

"Well, they did," she says, turning around to raise her eyebrows at me. As she turns back to the sink, the wet glass she is holding slips from her fingers—in the blink of an eye she is squatting like a baseball catcher and catching the glass just before it hits the kitchen tiles.

"Nice save," I say, swallowing a chip too quickly, the edge scratching my throat.

I'm *not* jealous of Honey's leining. But I think what has also been scratching my throat is that where I see roadblocks, she sees different routes, or that a roadblock might really only be those orange traffic cones that can simply be picked up and moved away.

"Are you nervous to lein?" I ask.

"A bit," she admits. "But Naomi says to imagine I am a queen wearing a crown. She says it's a public-speaking trick her dad taught her but that it works well for leining too."

"You're going to be great," I say, and I really do mean it. I have no doubt she's going to knock it out of the ballpark. Like she always does.

"Thanks, Milla," she says. Then I tell her about the issue with my mother and which dress to wear to Natalie's and show her the pictures on my phone. "They're both really nice," she says.

"But I'd rather wear the peach one to Natalie's. If we do the best friend's speech, everyone will be looking at us—it's going to be a really fancy party and the peach dress is the fanciest."

"But your mother chose it as your bat mitzvah dress. You want to wear your bat mitzvah dress to Natalie's bat mitzvah before you've worn it to your own?"

"I don't want it to be my bat mitzvah dress!" I say. "That's the thing." Honey looks at me mildly. "I mean, I really like it, but it's just not what I had in mind for my bat mitzvah."

"And . . . ?"

"And, you were unhappy when you didn't like what you were doing for your bat mitzvah."

"That was because I wanted to lein. This is about a dress."

"Well, they're in the pictures forever!" I cry, even though that's not the point. But I can't put into words what the point really is: It's about the dress, but not about the dress. It's about inside and outside choices! And choosing for myself. I would think Honey, of all people, would understand that. I know I'm lucky to have so many dresses. Why is she making me sound petty and spoiled?

Honey raises her eyebrows.

"Forget it," I say.

My mother wins, and I lay out the pale blue dress to wear to Natalie's bat mitzvah. Right after Shabbat, Tali and Sophie come over, and we get ready together. Sophie blow-dries my hair and then curls it into big waves with a curling iron she got for her bat mitzvah. Tali has brought a makeup kit she got for *her* bat mitzvah and does all our makeup.

"I've been watching videos," she says as she deftly

opens its drawers to find me the right blush. I look at Sophie expertly wielding her curling iron. They are both wearing the dresses they wore to their bat mitzvahs.

"Hey, I have an idea," I tell them. "Why don't you trade sashes for tonight? That way you'll look a little different from your own parties?" Their faces light up, and they wordlessly reach behind themselves to untie their bows and hand them to the other. I feel my face light up too. "And how about instead of wearing it in a bow, you can tie it like this—" I demonstrate on Tali what I think is a more sophisticated knot, settling it to the front and slightly off-center.

"Ooh, do mine," Sophie says as Tali admires herself in the mirror.

"Sure!" I say, swiftly doing Sophie's tie and nudging it to the opposite side from how I did Tali's.

"C'mon, girls!" my dad hollers, and we tumble down the stairs and into the car, giggling in the back seat the whole way.

When we get there, two coachmen open the doors for us, and when we enter the hotel lobby, we are handed fancy glittery masks to hold against our faces with a stick. The music is pulsing, and Natalie rushes over to greet us, sweeping me, Tali, and Sophie into the exciting atmosphere. The party becomes a whir. Dancers from a famous troupe appear, and Natalie puts on a gold leotard and performs with them. There's no best friend's speech: Natalie told us last week that her parents aren't having any speeches at all—they think they're boring! Instead there is a video of celebrities wishing Natalie "Mazal Tov" on her bat mitzvah. There is a real DJ, and a band, and all the kids in my class dance—me, Tali, and Sophie too—jumping up and down in one big circle. I keep finding myself next to Noam in the heaving huddle, and I wonder if it is just coincidence. Then, out of the corner of my eye, I see my *mother* dancing in a huddle with some other mothers. We all agree this is *extremely* embarrassing and that we should try as hard as we can *not* to look!

Everyone seems to be having an awesome time.

Does that mean that, despite Natalie's family always showing off their money, a lot of people still like them? I think about my relationship with Natalie: She gets on my nerves sometimes, but it wouldn't be truthful to say I don't enjoy spending time with her. I didn't like it when it felt like she was trying to steal Honey from me. But looking back, I can see she probably just wanted to make sure she wasn't going to be left out. If Tali and Sophie are best friends, and me and Honey are best friends—but Honey wasn't in our school, so me, Natalie, Sophie, and Tali were a foursome—it would make sense that with Honey suddenly there, Natalie was worried she would be a fifth wheel.

Anyway, Natalie Aronovich's bat mitzvah is definitely an extravagant affair, but nothing too wild happens. I flutter around all night with my friends, dancing and laughing at all the different entertainment booths. It's too bad Honey isn't here. She's missed out on a really fun party. But then I think: Honey probably really doesn't care.

CHAPTER 12

RIGHT SIDE UP

The next day, my mother prints out an e-vite and pins it to the bulletin board in the kitchen.

With gratitude to Hashem, it is our honor to invite you to join a special women's Megillas Esther reading on the 14th day of the Jewish month of Adar, Purim eve, 6:30 p.m., basement meeting hall of Congregation Ohav Shalom, where our dear daughter Hencha will, G-d willing, celebrate her Bas Mitzvah.

I smile to myself at the incongruity of the wording—the Wines using the more traditional Ashkenazi pronunciation of *"bas"* rather than "bat" about Honey doing something so edgy and modern as leining megillah at a women's service. She really is brave to have decided to do this, and to have actually managed to convince her family. Only Honey, I think, shaking my head at my friend.

"Good luck," I mouth to Honey later that week, waving

wildly as soon as my mom and Aunty Steph and I enter the bright basement meeting hall on Purim eve.

Purim is definitely the most fun of all the Jewish holidays. We bake jam-filled hamantaschen cookies, deliver food baskets to our friends, give charity, and dress up in costumes. My favorite part is hearing the megillah, the Purim story, which talks about "v'nahafoch hu," or things being turned around. In the story, evil Haman devised an amazing reward for King Achashveyrosh to honor a most-loyal adviser— thinking that adviser would be himself—but instead it went to Mordechai the Jew, Queen Esther's uncle. And instead of the Jewish people getting destroyed, they were saved. Anyway, not only is Purim super fun, but it makes us Orthodox kids feel less weird about the fact that we don't celebrate Halloween.

Honey is already sitting up front with her mother, Miriam, Aaron, Dan-Dan, her grandmother, Aginéni, and Susie. Naomi Dayan is standing with another woman at a large lectern where the megillah has already been placed. I try not to make eye contact with Aginéni. What if she yells at me for not coming over to visit her yet? Honey grins and gives me a thumbs-up, gesturing for us to find a seat in the quickly filling room.

It is not exactly weird to be sitting in shul with only women, because the women always sit together—but it is really weird that there is no men's section. Looking around the room, bathed in unflattering basement fluorescent lighting, there are rows and rows of ladies and girls. Some are dressed up in full costumes, and some are wearing funny accessories, like silly hats or headbands with antennae. Aunty Steph has drawn me a rainbow next to one eye and a peace sign next to my other eye with face paint. A few relatives told Mr. and Mrs. Wine that they would *never* attend a women's megillah reading, *under any circumstances*, because they didn't think it was really Orthodox. But there are still a bunch of them sitting at the back, with thick orangey cover-up and rouged cheeks, the brims of their extravagantly decorated felt hats overlapping as they bend their heads to one another to whisper. I hope it's not about Honey.

Naomi raps the table lightly for silence. The woman standing next to her begins with the special blessings for reading the megillah and then starts to chant the first chapter from the scroll in a high and melodic voice. I keep my head down toward my booklet and follow along.

Crash.

Aginéni's cane has fallen down with a crack against the stone floor, and the woman reading from the megillah pauses. I scratch at something on my cheek and catch the top of Josh Wine's face peering through the high square window in the top of the metal door and then Micah's face pressed against the bottom window. I stifle a laugh. Mr. Wine and Honey's brothers, and actually Shmuel Yosef too, are hanging around outside in the hallway so they can hear Honey through the door when it's her turn. Miriam leans down to pick up the cane for Aginéni. The reading resumes.

Finally, Honey approaches the bima quietly, Dan-Dan's pink plastic tiara perched at a deliberately jaunty angle on her golden hair, a purple cape over her shoulders. Even I, her best friend, do a double take and big *shshshshs* erupt from all directions. Honey looks like a queen about to address her subjects. She takes her spot in front of the scroll, and the room falls silent. Naomi Dayan points to the spot where the chapter begins. Then Honey launches into her leining the same way she plays basketball, baseball, or anything she wants to win: fast, graceful, steady, and strong. I glance over at my mother. Instead of looking in her book, she is looking at Honey, her face rapt.

Honey is leining the third chapter, which is the first time Haman's name is mentioned, and when she gets to it, the room goes wild with everyone's noisemakers drowning out the evil Haman's name. Mrs. Wine holds Aaron's head in her lap, covering his ear with one arm while silently shaking a castanet with the other. My mother stomps her feet, and Aunty Steph rings a cowbell. The Wine men blow a horn from outside the door. I make my noisy gragger go crackling round and round. I might be trying to boo Haman, but all I can think of is that I am cheering for Honey. It feels like everyone here is doing the same.

When she has read the last word of her chapter, Honey looks up and our eyes catch. She grins and gives me a thumbs-up, and the room laughs and lots of women turn back to me or strain forward to see who Honey was signaling. Everyone starts singing and clapping for Honey. As she makes her way back to her seat, I feel so proud of her and proud that she *is* really my best friend, even if I don't get to make a best friend's speech for her. I scratch my cheek again. At Natalie's bat mitzvah, Natalie was a princess. But even in a cheap plastic kid's crown, Honey is a queen. It's not v'nahafoch hu—that things have been turned around—it's just simply revealed what was there all along. I guess Tali, Sophie, Rivkie, Natalie, and Honey—even Tammy—all had the right bat mitzvah for them.

After the megillah reading ends, I hang back to hug Honey, but she is surrounded in an impenetrable circle of family, including the big-hatted ladies. So I head to the back of the room, where a partition has been pulled aside to reveal a kiddush-type spread sponsored by the Wines, with tables swarmed by kids grabbing pastries and adults pouring themselves shots of liquor. I see Josh already holding two full plates aloft and making his way toward Aaron, who has climbed onto a stack of chairs in the corner. Before I reach the tables though, a finger taps my shoulder from behind. I turn around to see Aginéni looking at me keenly.

"So, nu, are you going to do this too?" she says without saying hello, and sweeps her arm around the room to the lectern. "Is this for you?"

I scratch my cheek. "Um—"

"What?" she says, leaning forward on her cane.

"Probably not," I say, shuffling my feet.

"Hmm. Well, just because you haven't done something yet doesn't mean you never will."

"I guess," I say.

"You haven't come to see me."

"Oh. Um—" I look helplessly at the end of the room, where Aunty Steph and Shmuel Yosef are sharing a plate of hamantaschen. I notice Aginéni is wearing a butterfly pin with pink sparkling jewels in the wings. "Yeah," I say, before turning my attention to the floor. My face is burning. I rub my cheek again, still keeping my eyes down.

"Yes, well, that's not to say you never will. Or that you'll never want to," she says, and I feel her gaze on me, its energy forcing me to look directly at her. Reluctantly I raise my eyes and realize with a start that she's holding in a smile.

"I see you like my brooch." She points to her butterfly pin, and I nod shyly. "My dear Imre-batchi had a costume jewelry business. So you see, this is my *costume* for Purim. It's my little joke with myself."

I let out a squeaky laugh. Her eyes are twinkling. "I have boxes and boxes of the dreck," she says. "My dear

Imre-batchi was a terrible businessman. If you ever want something for yourself, to complement an outfit or give yourself a little sparkle, be my guest. But it means you have to come over."

She turns away, leaning heavily on her cane, and starts moving toward the schnapps table. Ezra breaks away from where he's standing with Josh and Aaron and takes Aginéni's arm, helping her along. She shakes it loose and turns back to me. "And tell your mother to take a look at your face. I think you're having an allergic reaction to that chazerai painted on it."

Later that night, as I am putting cortisone cream on my hives before I go to bed, I look at myself in the mirror and think about what Aginéni asked me: *Are you going to do this too? Is this for you?*

I do in fact like the idea of standing at a lectern.

Just not for leining.

CHAPTER 13
ORANGE JUICE

"Milla-babe, forgive me, but I don't think your head's in the game today."

"Hmm?" I say, glancing back from the window. It's Shabbat afternoon, and Aunty Steph is looking at me, one finger on the verse in the Book of Ruth that we are working on. I'm not learning to lein Megillat Rut; we are studying the story and commentaries in honor of my bat mitzvah, and I'll make a speech about it at my party. But right now, I have another speech on my mind.

"It feels like maybe you're not so engaged with our learning," she says. She closes the book, leaving her finger inside to mark the page.

"No, it's fine," I say guiltily. "It's just that the speech contest at school is coming up, and I can't think of a topic."

"I told you, Milla, do feminism," my mother calls from the kitchen, where she's cleaning up from lunch and eavesdropping. She comes to stand in the doorway of the den, where Aunty Steph and I are learning. "Or antisemitism. It's good to do an ism."

"What's an ism?" Max says, looking up from the Lego he's building on the floor with Shmuel Yosef.

"It's the belief in something," my mom answers.

"How about atheism?" suggests Shmuel Yosef, who has taken to sleeping at the Wines' and joining us for Shabbat lunch—and the whole afternoon—whenever Aunty Steph is with us.

"It's just, I want to do something really different," I say. "Something big."

"Believing in something is big," my mother says, shooting Shmuel Yosef a withering glance. There's a knock on the door, and she goes to get it.

"Hey, Sugaree," Aunty Steph says to Honey as she joins us on the couch. "Do you know what you're doing for the speech contest yet?"

"Not yet," Honey says. "I'm hoping inspiration will strike soon." Everyone laughs.

I am also hoping for inspiration. Yesterday Mr. Sandler explained the way it works: Everyone in the middle school has to prepare a speech, four to five minutes long. Starting two Mondays from now, each person will present their speech to their class over the course of one week. At the end of the week, we vote for our top three choices in our class. The next week, on Monday, the three people do their speeches again, and the class votes on whose they think is best, second best, and third best. The first best speech will be the class's representative at the big middle school speech contest.

Last year, we got to be in the audience. It was very dramatic. A girl said her first sentence three times and then ran off the stage crying. Someone's mother stood up and shouted, "Moishy, you're not enunciating, start again!" Another girl spoke with what my mother calls "poise" in a way that seemed otherworldly to me. The judges, of which my mother was one, chose her as the winner.

"How about something sports related?" suggests Shmuel Yosef. "Like, 'Everything I Know About the World I Know from Snooker'?"

My mother rolls her eyes.

"What's snooker?" Honey, Max, and I say at the same time.

"It's like pool," Shmuel Yosef says, as if that should clear things up. My mother's eyeballs roll all the way into her head and might require a search party to retrieve them.

"With the eight ball and the cues," my dad supplies, joining my mom in the doorway. Shmuel Yosef mimes something unintelligible. "But, actually," my dad says, "it's a good idea—just pick your favorite sport—hockey, baseball . . . badminton." My dad winks.

"That could be good for you, Sugaree," my aunt says, looking adoringly at Shmuel Yosef.

"Yeah, that's not bad," agrees Honey.

"Yes," my mom interjects. "But—not to be glib—it's the isms that always win. You know, like—" She pauses as she glances at Aunty Steph and Shmuel Yosef looking deep into each other's eyes and flashes a not-so-subtle face at my father. She cannot handle what she calls the "goo-goo eyes." Me and Honey look at each other and smirk.

"What's so funny?" Max says.

"Oh, your mommy, she's just so silly," my dad says with a straight face.

"She is?" Max says, bewildered.

"Jonathan, even Max knows I am the least silly person alive!" my mother says indignantly, leaning over to whack my father's arm. "And in all seriousness, Milla, you should do feminism for your speech. I can help you with it!"

"One year, this girl in my class did her speech on how to peel an orange," Aunty Steph says, turning away from Shmuel Yosef's face and toward the rest of us. "It was super cool."

An image of a mandarin orange pops into my head and how my grandfather in Israel peels it in one long curling strip. My mother refuses to peel oranges with her bare fingers and wears latex gloves because she hates when her hands smell like oranges. Ezra Wine cuts the peel in big slabs with a knife and then carefully pushes the glistening sections out of their skin and into a salad. I wonder if you could tell something about a person from the way they peel an orange. Suddenly, I wish Shabbat was over so I can run up to my room, turn on the computer, and start writing my speech already.

I have my topic.

The rest of the afternoon, we hang out with Aunty Steph and Shmuel Yosef in the den, and I'm sure we talk about lots of interesting things, but I have no idea what they are because all I am doing is writing my speech inside my head. And thinking of good lines and what the order of everything should be.

By Sunday night, I have the whole thing written out, and by Monday night, I begin practicing it out loud to myself in my room, a show playing on my laptop in the background so no one can hear me.

I practice my speech every night, changing some words here and there, memorizing it. On Thursday after school, I do it in front of the mirror for the first time and have to peer in closer to make sure it is me. I see someone who is waving her arms in demonstration, moving her mouth and eyebrows in all kinds of expression, and using her voice to go up and down to make good points. In short, it does not look like the Milla Bloom I know. But when I finish the four minutes and forty-five seconds of my speech, I smile right back at her.

I'm so busy that I hardly talk to any of my friends that week, even Honey. But we make a plan to go to Starbucks after school on Friday. It's still freezing cold out, but slowly the days have been getting longer and it's getting dark later—which means Shabbat doesn't start so early anymore. Until Passover though, school ends at one p.m. on Fridays, and it's nice to have the afternoon to ourselves. As soon as we walk in, Honey nudges me hard.

"Ow," I say, rubbing my shoulder. She inclines her head, and I follow her gaze to a man standing by the counter. He's tall and has dark wavy hair.

"Mr. Sandler!" Honey shouts, dragging me by my jacket to where he's standing. All of Starbucks turns to look at us, and I feel mortified. I hate when Honey doesn't notice—or care—that she's making a spectacle of us.

"Milla, Honey—" Mr. Sandler says with a big smile. "How are you?"

"Baruch Hashem, we're good," Honey says, before I can answer for myself. "How are you?"

"I'm good too," Mr. Sandler says. "Thank you for asking. So, you kids ready for the speech contest on Monday?"

"Yup!" Honey says while I nod shyly. The Starbucks is stifling hot with steam on the windows, and I'm starting to sweat inside my ski jacket. Mr. Sandler's tie is loosened, and he's rolled up his shirtsleeves. Behind him, I see a laptop open on a table, notebooks, and a navy peacoat over the chair.

"Well, I'm sure you'll each make your speech your

own," Mr. Sandler says. "You know, there are only so many stories in the universe, but how you tell them is what makes each one unique."

"Oh, mine is unique, all right," Honey says eagerly, and I hope he doesn't ask us what our topics are. Whatever Honey's topic is, I know she's going to make it amazing.

"How about you, Milla?" Mr. Sandler says, turning to me with that smile that makes me feel like he's including me in his universe, where I can accomplish anything I put my mind to.

"Mine is unique too," I say, smiling back.

"Excellent," he says, his eyes twinkling. "I'm sure you'll both do great. By the way, Milla, I marked your essay on heroes in myths and legends last night—*very* incisive—you showed really sophisticated critical and creative thinking."

I feel my face flush with pleasure. I'd worked hard on that essay.

"That's my Milla," Honey says, putting her arm around me. I squirm in an unfamiliar way. *Her* Milla?

"William!" the barista hollers in the background.

"Coming!" Mr. Sandler calls back. "My Starbucks name," he says to us with a wink before he ambles toward the counter. "Bye, kids. Good luck. Do yourselves proud. That's always the best you can hope for."

After lunch on Shabbat, I call Max into my room and do my speech in front of him. He laughs his head off at all the right times. "You're funny, Milla," he says afterward.

"Thanks, Max," I say, smiling.

On Sunday, my mother knocks on my door. I've been in my room all day. "Do you want to do a practice run?" she asks me.

"No, it's okay."

"Milla, you don't want to look unprepared. It's bad enough you're doing such a silly topic."

"I'm prepared" is all I say.

Mr. Sandler is taking one person from the top of the alphabet and one person from the bottom to make the order of speech presentations for our class, so me being "B" and Honey being "W," we both have to do our speeches on the first day, Monday.

Honey goes first. As she walks up to the front of the room, Noam and Eitan sing this song people have been singing about her lately, *"Sugar, na-na, na-na, na-na, ah, honey, honey,*" but she ignores them. She turns to us and stands straight, stares right, stares left, stares center, and then says in a loud voice:

"Have you ever noticed how people just don't know how to peel oranges properly?"

Huh?

"Do *you* know how to peel an orange?" Honey asks our class, pointing her finger and scanning it across the room.

What?

My shoulders go all funny.

Even though oranges are all I have been thinking about day and night, I didn't speak to Honey about our speeches. I can't say why exactly, because even though I did get the idea from Aunty Steph, the speech is all my own imagination. But I still haven't talked about it.

I tune back in to hear what Honey is saying.

"Did you know that there are certain *dos* and certain *don'ts* to peeling an orange? Well, have no fear, because *I* am here to tell you what they are."

My heart gallops against my ribs, and my face feels cold.

I am an orange in the bottom of the crate: bright

and shiny and bumpy last night, fuzzed with white and green mold this morning.

I grip the orange I brought as a prop.

How could she do this to me?

It's no more your idea than hers, a little voice inside my head defends her. I push it aside. I am too busy thinking about how I am now supposed to get up in front of my whole class and also do a speech about peeling oranges.

Okay, I think, trying to get control of my breathing. Okay. Okay. Mine is different enough from hers. At least what I can hear of what Honey is actually saying. I am having trouble concentrating.

All I can think about is that when it's my turn all everyone will be thinking is *Whah? Another speech on the same topic!* And this time, this time by yours truly: the quieter, lesser, regular citizen versus the celebrity that is Honey Wine.

I can already hear Eric's "humph" before I even start. I grip my orange so tightly I'm surprised it doesn't squirt all over me. I feel like my face is covered in juice anyway.

Mr. Sandler is nodding and smiling as he watches Honey. I feel like someone has ripped out a piece of me.

When Honey is done, she flashes me a grin. I look away. She lifts her shoulders in a question mark, but Mr. Sandler has called me up and I find myself in front of the class holding my orange.

Right on cue, Eric calls, "More freshly squeezed orange juice, anyone?" and everyone laughs. My mouth is dry, and everything is tingling. I stare at the tops of the heads of all the kids in my class. I swallow. I'm not sure I'm breathing.

But I fight the urge to finger the ends of my braids. I flick one and then the other over my shoulders instead.

I clear my throat and count to three in my head.

"Friends, classmates, teacher: You might not know this, but I am here to tell you that the way you peel an orange says a lot about *you*."

I hold up my orange. "My grandpa—he has time, he has experience, he has patience. He whittles it in one long strip. He says it's more satisfying to enjoy the inside when the outside has been taken care of properly. My twin toddler cousins, on the other hand, they have no experience in life, or patience—" I pretend to bite the orange whole like you would an apple. Everyone laughs.

I pause, suddenly realizing that I'm doing this. In front of an audience. It's like I heard my voice just now—but it's hard to connect that it was me, standing up here in front of everybody, that I was hearing.

But I am not going to get freaked out. I am not going to think about what (else) can go wrong. I am giving my speech now, how I practiced it, and in the best way I can.

I take another deep breath.

"A Talmudic discussion," I say, pretending to stroke my beard like a rabbi. "The House of Hillel says we should peel from left to right, but the House of Shammai says we should peel from right to left." Everyone laughs again.

"The couple-in-love peel?" I pretend to make goo-goo eyes at another person, my face all moony as I peel my orange without looking at it. I do a fancy-lady peel, a military peel, and a bus-driver peel, pretending to throw the peel out the window. Everyone is laughing at all the right moments. Just where I planned for them to, where I wanted them to. I can hear Mr. Sandler's loud guffaws.

When I pause for dramatic effect like my mom does, the class is so still, staring right at me, all I can hear is Eitan Moses's heavy breathing. And when I finish in exactly four minutes and forty-five seconds, just like I practiced, everyone bursts out clapping. They are looking at me like I am a different Milla Bloom than I was four minutes and forty-five seconds earlier.

When I walk back to my seat, Honey smiles at me, but it isn't the big grin from before.

CHAPTER 14
ORANGE CRUSH

The rest of the day it is the elephant in the room. All Mr. Sandler said when I was done was "Two different takes on the same subject. That's art, that's life." But I can't bring myself to say anything light or funny or anything at all to Honey about us both doing a peeling-an-orange speech, and she doesn't say anything to me either. It feels like the elephant is not just in the room but sitting on my head.

As we are at our lockers packing up, Natalie says, "So, I gotta know: Who stole the idea from who? You guys should've done the speech together once you had the same topic." She laughs.

"We're best friends, not the same person," I say as Honey narrows her eyes and gives Natalie a death stare.

"No one stole anything from anyone," Honey says.

"Oh yeah, no, of course not," Natalie backpedals. "I just thought it was funny. Well, anyway, you were both really good. In your own way and all."

Honey and I sit next to each other in silence the whole bus ride home.

"It *is* kind of funny, Milla," Honey finally says as we are getting off the bus. "And like Mr. Sandler said, it might be the same topic but we do it really differently."

"I guess," I say.

She looks like she's waiting for me to say something else, but when I don't, she shrugs and starts walking toward our houses. I follow her. I can tell she is kind of mad at me too, but what can either of us say to the other? Natalie was just trying to stir things up like she always does; Honey and I both know that neither of us stole the other's totally original creative idea. Neither of us even claimed dibs on it when Aunty Steph mentioned the peeling-an-orange speech. But still. I feel like Honey did in fact steal something from me. Does she always need to hog the limelight?

We continue to walk in silence. It will be Passover in a few weeks, but the weather can't decide if it is ready for spring yet. Honey has her ski jacket tied around her waist, and I have my windbreaker zipped up to my chin. We say goodbye when we get to my house and I turn to wave from my front door because I always do, but she is sprinting away toward her house and she doesn't see me.

I am surprised by the knob of angry feeling, hard like a baseball, lodged in my chest.

The rest of the week, we listen to everyone else's speeches. On Friday, we vote for the best three and Mr. Sandler reveals the results at the end of class: Noam ("Everything You Need to Know in Life You Can Learn from a Game of Basketball"), Honey ("The Dos and Don'ts of Peeling an Orange"), and me ("How Are You Peeling?"). We each have to do our speech again on Monday. I want to be excited—well, I *am* excited—but it doesn't fill me up the way I thought it would. It is laced with something sour.

As Honey and I make our way off the bus home, a bunch of kids at the back sing, *"Honey, na-na, na-na, na-na, ah, ORANGE, ORANGE."*

"Get a life already," Honey says to them, turning back for a minute before she steps off. But suddenly I feel like I can't take it anymore. The baseball is rising into my throat. And I can't swallow.

"Why are you looking at me like that?" Honey says to me.

I wait until we reach the sidewalk, and then I tell her, "Why can't you let me have my own thing for once?"

"What are you talking about, Milla?" She pushes the sleeves of Josh's varsity jacket up. She somehow makes not having her own spring jacket look cool. "So we have the same speech topic—okay, it's ridiculous—but it's not the same speech, so it is what it is. It's actually kind of funny."

"No, it isn't," I say. "It's sad. Why do you always feel like you have to win everything? Everyone loves you already. Everyone already thinks you're great. Why can't I win something for once?"

She stares at me. "You might, Milla. Your speech is really good."

"Whatever," I say.

"What's wrong with you?" she asks. She looks genuinely surprised.

"What's wrong with you?" I challenge. It doesn't even make sense, but I don't care. I want to throw this baseball of anger right in her face.

"Milla, not everybody refuses to participate in things they think they might not be good at."

"What's that supposed to mean?" I say.

We have been walking, but now she stops and steps toward me. I stand still. We are about the same height, but I don't look directly at her.

"It means you can't just give up and cry when you think you don't have a chance, or at the first sign that things aren't perfect. What's the point of only doing things you already know you're good at?"

"The point," I spit. "The point is that when you're friends with someone, you're supposed to care about their feelings, not just about impressing everyone all the time."

She was calm before, but now her whole body juts forward. "I care more about your feelings than you ever do about mine!" she shouts. "And you're like that with everybody. If it's ever about one person, that person is always *you*."

"What are you talking about?" I shout back. She has never spoken to me like this before.

"How do you think it feels to know that my best friend, who comes over all the time, couldn't care less if I'm home or not, as long as Micah, or my mother, or anyone else is there?"

"That's not true!" I cry. I take a step back as if she has pushed me. I want to say that I come for both: her and her family. The baseball is out now, and my chest feels funny.

"And then"—she pauses and fixes her eyes right on mine so I have no choice but to meet them—"and then you complain about your own mother nonstop, but you're the one who's horrible to her!"

I take another step back and stumble on a clump of mud. What is Honey saying to me? She is flinging my mother at me like a weapon she's been keeping in her pocket. Since when does she feel this way?

"You don't know anything about my mother!" I say.

"No, I do!" she says. "I'd be mad at you too if I was her. She never asks you to help with anything, and you just sit there and let her do things for you and buy things for you like it's your right. And you don't even say thank you!"

"I do too say thank you!" I say, stamping my foot onto the muddy grass, soggy and yellow from melted snow. "But everything has to be her way—she never asks me what *I* want!"

"Milla, do you think my mother has taken me on shopping sprees so I can have a different dress to wear to every party I go to plus some for spare, just in case I change my mind?"

I hesitate. It's not a secret that Honey's grandparents pay for her to go to camp and her school fees too. And even though my family's definitely not rich-rich like Natalie's, I know we are what Aunty Steph calls "privileged."

"But—but she only buys what she thinks is nice—it's never what I actually want," I say. And how can I explain to Honey the look on my mother's face when she was leining?

Honey rolls her eyes. Her mouth is set. She doesn't get the difference. Like my mother. She's making me sound selfish and unappreciative.

How typical: *I* am the one who's mad at her, but *she's* taken charge of the argument. Honey has started walking again, and I have to take fast steps to catch up with her.

"Fine, be on her side!" I scream. We are at my driveway, but she just keeps going. I stomp up my front walk and don't even turn to wave goodbye, not that she would see me anyway since she is already halfway down the street. I slam the front door, run up to my room, and slam that door too.

"No slamming doors!" my mother yells from the kitchen. *They can have each other*, I think, and burst into tears.

On Shabbat, neither Honey nor I walk over to the other's house. When Shabbat is over, we don't call each other. I text Natalie, but she doesn't reply.

Then she writes, *on w noam try me later.*

And then, *he says 2 tell u he says hi haha.*

Oh, haha, tell him to text me, I write.

Lol, I write, after a while. *You still on with N?*

My phone stays silent all night even though I turned up the volume.

On Sunday, I stay in my room and practice my speech over and over again. I look in the mirror, and I think about the terrible things Honey said to me.

Of course I'm shy, but that doesn't mean I never want to be noticed. That doesn't mean I always want to stand in Honey's shadow. I don't mind her taking center stage for most things; that's the way she is. It's fine with me. But I'm not "*her* Milla." And it is not true that I don't take part in things I think I'm going to fail at; I would just rather save putting myself out there for the things that really matter to me. Like this stupid speech contest.

When I think about it, yes, it *is* kind of funny that we are doing the same speech topic. And I know it isn't fair to not want her to do a good job on her speech just because I want to shine with mine, but that is what I want.

I drop my eyes to my feet. I can't look at my face after having that thought.

But how dare she bring my mother into this—and be on her side! I look back at my face and go through my speech again.

On Monday, it seems like the whole school is singing *"Honey, na-na, na-na, na-na, ah, ORANGE, ORANGE,"* or *"Sugar, na-na, na-na, na-na, ah, ORANGE, ORANGE"* when they see either of us. I am in the hallway on the way to the bathroom when two seventh-grade boys block my path and sing it at me.

"Who's going to win?" one of them says. "Honey or Sugar?"

I have never hated a song so much in my life.

"It's going to be orange crush, that's for sure!" the other guy says. They slap each other on the back and crack up. My rubber soles squeak on the floor as I rush away.

At recess, I go back to the bathroom. I can't bear to be in the schoolyard and see who is going to huddle with who. I am sitting on the radiator whispering my speech to myself when the door bangs open.

"I thought I'd find you here," Honey says. She stands with her hands on her hips. "I just wanted to say good luck. May the best one win."

"Thanks," I mumble, looking down. Tears come to my eyes every time I remember her telling me off in front of my house. The whole morning, I have kept myself from looking at her. But of course, Honey is Honey and can still have it in her to go and find me and wish me good luck even though we are in a fight and competing against each other. I know I am being small, but I do not have it in me to wish her good luck back. I focus on a piece of toilet paper on the floor. I can hear her breathing, waiting for me to say something. I look up and am startled by the hurt expression nakedly on her face. I lose my balance and slide off the radiator, and before I can stammer anything out, the door bangs shut behind her.

This time, I go first. I say my speech without a hitch. Even though I feel a bit silly doing all the dramatic things over again in front of everybody, like it somehow feels fake and scripted, I do it anyway with all I have, and everyone laughs again in all the right places. I get a huge applause from my class and I feel like their clapping hands are patting me on the back. Then comes Honey. She is pretty funny too. But I notice her speech is actually a little different from the first time, and it doesn't sound quite as good. People laugh, but more like chuckles at her performance and the strange things she is doing. At one point, she looks like she's forgotten what she is supposed to say and so instead she does a little dance and calls it the "peeling-an-orange shimmy."

Oh, Honey, I realize to myself. *You never even wrote it out in full; you've just been winging it.* For once, she doesn't entirely get away with it. When the class votes again, she comes in last.

Noam comes in second.

I am going to represent our class at the middle school speech contest.

CHAPTER 15

SOMETHING SPARKLY

I can't believe it. Neither can my mother. After dinner, she has me pull up a chair to the dark alcove at the back of the kitchen where her workstation is so she can show me a video on "power poses," which are ways to stand to give you more confidence.

"Just remember, Milla," she says, "you can 'fake it till you make it.'"

I thought I had already made it.

Isn't she proud of me for getting to the speech contest?

"Don't give me that vinegar face, Milla Ruth," she says. "I'm not saying anything insulting. But if you really want to win, you need to know the battle is just beginning. You don't want to leave anything to chance." She pauses, as if she's hesitating on whether or not she should say something. "Milla, have you thought about why you think your speech deserves to win?"

"What?" *What kind of question is that?* "Uh, because it's good? I think, anyway."

"Yes." She looks uncomfortable. "But what makes it good? If you want, I can talk it through with you."

"Mom—" I say.

Her cell phone rings. "Oh, wait, it's the tent guys for your bat mitzvah." Her face is torn.

"Take it," I say in as steady a voice as I can. I look at the woman on the screen doing the power poses. I think about Honey in her cape and tiara.

She nods. "We'll pick this up later," she says, pointing to herself and then to me.

"Whatever," I say under my breath, and stalk out of the kitchen, almost running into Max.

"Hi, Milla, wanna play?"

"Sorry, Max, I need to practice my speech." He's dressed as a space ranger and flying his Lego airplane. "Remember, the big contest is next week."

"Don't worry, Milla," he tells me. "You're going to be great!"

"Thanks, Max. At least someone believes in me."

All week, Honey and I avoid each other. I am working on a science project with Natalie, which is a disaster because both of us are awful at science, but that means I go home with her most days after school. And

Honey is doing intramural volleyball during lunch and has joined an ongoing seventh-grade kickball game during recess. I also do a lot of practicing by myself in the quiet of my bedroom. Having a great speech and performing it perfectly—isn't that what it takes to deserve to win?

On Sunday morning, I am standing in front of the mirror, working on getting my hand motions just right for a new bit I've added about how my mother peels oranges for Max wearing latex gloves, when I stop and look at myself. Fuzzy sweatpants. Brown curlyish hair in braids. Something that could be a pimple emerging on my forehead. I take out my braids and shake out my hair. I stand in front of my closet for a while looking at my clothes, trying to decide what I should wear to the contest. I go back in front of the mirror. And then I realize what I need.

A caretaker answers the door. "Mrs. Isaacovich, you have a visitor," she calls back toward the kitchen. "What's your name, darling?" she asks me.

"Milla—Milla Bloom."

"It's Milla Bloom," she calls back again.

"Who?" comes the voice from the kitchen.

"Um, hi, um, Aginéni," I call, stumbling over my words. "Uh, it's me—Milla—the girl who likes to read?" My face is bright red.

"Oh, *you*. You came. Well done."

"Yeah, um—"

"So, nu, come in."

The caretaker smiles, ushering me into the kitchen before disappearing to the back of the house.

"Hi," I say. Aginéni is sitting at the Formica table with a glass of tea, reading a large hardcover book with a magnifying glass. Before I lose my nerve, I blurt out why I've come. "So remember you said you had boxes of costume jewelry? And that if I ever needed something sparkly, I could borrow from you?"

"Yes," she says. "I did."

"Um, so. I need something sparkly."

She puts down the magnifying glass and gestures for me to sit on a chair at the table. She closes her book. *Most Likely To . . . Daisy*.

I smile. Then I take a breath and sit down. "I'm in a contest," I say by way of explanation.

"You don't think you're sparkly enough?"

"Not really." I shrug.

"Tell me about this contest."

I explain about the speech and the semifinals and now the finals.

"So you won, and you won again. Hmm." Aginéni's eyes are bright. "Your speech must be good. You must perform it well."

I nod shyly. "But I won against my best friend." I don't mention it's Honey. "And she's good at everything. Better than me. Everyone always pays attention to her. So I feel like they made a mistake in choosing me. And that I'm going to let my whole class down. And my parents. Especially my mom. She doesn't think my speech deserves to win." Everything's coming out in a rush, but Aginéni's eyes stay on mine. I look down at her library book.

"My mom keeps wanting to help me, giving me tips and stuff," I say. "But all she's doing is making it sound like her, not like me."

Aginéni cocks her head and takes a sip of her tea. "But you can do things by yourself." She smiles slyly. "You came here, didn't you?"

I nod.

"What?" she says.

"Yes," I mumble.

"Excuse me, perhaps my hearing is not so good?"

"Yes," I say clearly. "I did."

She's quiet then and takes another sip of her tea. When her eyes meet mine, I notice the veins and wrinkles around her eyelids. When she speaks again, her voice is softer, her accent thicker.

"I never got to be a mother. And my own mother I lost before I finished growing up. It shames me to admit, but I quarreled with her all the time. I had an opinion about everything, and she didn't care for my opinions. But what I wouldn't give to have one more minute with her. Soon I'll join her in shamayim. Along with my dear Imre-batchi and my brothers and sisters, my friends, all gone. Now I am all alone."

I am afraid to say anything. We sit in silence, and I think of the pink rose I saw growing in Aginéni's backyard last time I was here. I wonder if it made it through the winter, and if not, if it will come back soon now that it's almost spring.

"Mrs. Isaacovich, come, darling. It's time for your bath," the caretaker says, appearing at the kitchen doorway that leads to the back of the house.

Aginéni shoots daggers at her.

"I'm not your darling!" she says, her voice sharp.

But she pushes her chair away from the table and then leans on it to hoist herself up.

"Okay, sweetie," the caretaker says good-humoredly as she comes to take Aginéni's arm.

"It's good to have friends," Aginéni says to me, adjusting her pink turban and then clasping firmly to the caretaker's proffered arm. "But you can only be a truly good friend if you think of yourself to the same standard as you think of your friend. Friends aren't made to be statues you admire on a pedestal."

As she shuffles away, I think again with surprise at the wounded look on Honey's face in the bathroom when I didn't wish her good luck. Could it be that I can hurt her as easily as she can me? I wonder if Aginéni is right: that I want to see Honey as perfect and knowing everything and always in charge. I guess us being in a fight *has* made me see how much I rely on Honey for being that person.

When the screen door slams shut, I realize I never got to look in Aginéni's box of costume jewelry for a pin to wear to the contest.

CHAPTER 16

BLESSED IS THE TRUE JUDGE

The next morning, my dad is sitting at the kitchen table when I come down for breakfast. Usually, I don't see him in the mornings, or in the evenings, or during the week at all. Why is he still home? I go to give him a kiss on the cheek. He is wearing his yarmulke, which he doesn't wear when he's going to work.

"Dad, what's wrong?" I say when I see his face up close.

"Milla," he says, and pauses for a minute. He rubs his freshly shaved chin and looks at me. "I'm not sure how to tell you this. Raphi Sandler . . . He died. His funeral is this morning."

"What?" I say.

"Mr. Sandler had a heart attack yesterday." My dad's face is gray and pinched. "Milla, he's dead—" His voice cracks. "Baruch Dayan ha'Emet."

What?

My brain cannot compute what my dad has said.

Heart attack. Dead. Mr. Sandler? He has dark wavy hair with only a little gray in it. He has a booming voice. He has young children. I just saw him on Friday.

"I'm sorry, Milla," my dad says. He collects me into his arms, and I stand stiffly. It must be a mistake. Mr. Sandler will stride into class later this afternoon, put his hands up, and say, "Mea culpa, kids, just kidding. Here I am." My dad holds me tighter.

I think I'm supposed to cry, but all I can do is blink. I need to tell Honey.

My phone rings. It's Honey.

"Mr. Sandler—" she chokes.

"I know," I choke back.

At school, everyone is crying. Groups of kids sit in clumps on the floor with their backs against the lockers, their faces screwed up. As I pick my way through the hallway to find my friends, I see mascara like black calligraphy ink running down the cheeks of all the older girls. Tall boys with hoodies still on over their uniform shirts have the hoods pulled up over their heads. Everyone is hugging, and none of the teachers are even saying a thing about boys and girls not touching.

I still feel so shocked I just keep staring. I look at everyone crying and feel like I am floating above, watching them, watching myself. I don't want to have to share my sadness. How can I feel like I had a special connection to Mr. Sandler if all these people look like they feel the same way? Only Honey's shoulder, which I can sense next to mine throughout the day, reminds me that my feet are on the ground.

After school, Honey comes over and we head straight to the spare room. I lie down on the massage table, and she flicks on the Shabbat lamp, then sits cross-legged on the floor, her back against the bed. We are quiet. For the first time today, I suddenly remember that Honey and I have been in a fight and have barely spoken in a week. I stare at the ceiling where the pillar of light from the lamp creates eerie shadows. Usually, the small beam makes our thoughts feel more solemn, but this afternoon I think our thoughts are too solemn already, and the darkness is too heavy. I stand up and flip on the overhead light and then I fling myself onto the extra bed on my stomach with my face in my arms.

"It's just weird that we'll never see him again," Honey says after a while, and I want to cover my ears at the *final*-ness of those words. She's taken my place on the massage table. I turn to face her, my cheek on the pillow. "Even when we thought he left that time, at least there was the possibility of him coming back."

I swallow, wondering how Honey will take what I want to admit. "I know it's stupid, but I was upset he left that time because I wanted to be one of those kids that come to visit him when they're in high school, and he has them stand up in front of the class and he says, 'So-and-so was my superstar' or 'So-and-so was our class poet.'"

"He loved you, Milla," Honey says. "He always said your answers were 'impressive.'" She's taken out her ponytail, and her hair flows over the sides of the massage table.

"He said your answer about the red wheelbarrow was beautiful."

"Milla, that was only because I was trying to think like you and for once it worked! And remember what he said to you in Starbucks? About your 'incisive' essay."

"He won't get to see me at the speech contest—" I say, and then halt, wishing I could pull those words back, that I hadn't said that right now to Honey.

But she doesn't hesitate. "He loved your speech, Milla. You probably couldn't see as you were doing it, but he was laughing his head off. Everyone could tell he thought it was really creative."

"Yeah, but you had the same speech."

"It wasn't the same, Milla."

"I'm sorry we were in a fight," I say.

"Me too," she says quietly.

"I'm sorry I didn't wish you good luck," I say.

"It's okay," she says.

And then, like a storm flood crashing through house windows, I start sobbing and can't stop.

I weep and weep.

About everything.

After a while, Honey rolls over to her side. I feel her brown eyes studying me. I try to catch my breath. My tears have soaked the pillow, and I use the back of my hand to swipe at my nose.

"Should we pay a shiva call to his family?" she says. "I bet Ima would take us. She always says how important it is to be menachem avel and comfort people who are mourning. Anyway—" She wipes an eye with her sleeve. "It'll make us feel like we're doing something."

* * *

I was too little to remember when my zaidy died, and I have never been to a shiva house, where people come to comfort the mourners. My parents, who went to the Sandlers' yesterday, have always said a shiva house is not a place for children. But Mrs. Wine called my mom last night and they spoke for a while, and in the end, they agreed that in this case it was a good idea for us to go; they agreed that we are old enough.

Just as Honey and I are finishing supper, Josh, Ezra, and Micah come home from yeshiva, banging into the mudroom and through to the kitchen. Micah's face lights up when he sees me.

"Ooh, it's Milla!" he says. Josh salutes, and Ezra nods in my direction.

"I. SEE. DEAD. PEOPLE," Micah says, stalking toward me, looking to his brothers to join in. "I. SEE—"

I burst into tears.

"Micah!" Honey says with disgust.

"What? What did I do?" Micah says.

"Their teacher just died!" Josh supplies as Ezra looks menacingly at Micah.

"Oh," Micah says, his face reddening. "I didn't know! How was I supposed to know?"

Ezra digs into his pocket and hands me and Honey crumpled tissues. Honey isn't crying, but she doesn't look too good either. Sure, Mrs. Wine is on the chevra kadisha and the Wines talk about death matter-of-factly, but I don't think Honey has ever personally known anyone who's died before, or been to a shiva house. Josh comes over and gently bumps shoulders with her in protective solidarity.

I blow my nose. "No one tells me anything around here!" Micah mutters.

Mrs. Wine appears, adjusting her wig onto her head. "Come, girls, it's time." She smooths a wisp of hair from Honey's forehead, and with her other hand she rubs my back. "The mitzvah of comforting a mourner is so important because it's an act of kindness to both the living and the departed—a true chesed." She gives my back a final pat. "Come."

Mr. Sandler's house is in one of the new developments. When we finally find it, it looks like it might be carried away by ants. There are so many arms and heads and people overflowing its tiny, neat frame. There is no one else here our age, but there are more high school and college kids than at a music festival.

Mrs. Wine heads directly over to three people sitting on low chairs, their shirts torn as a Jewish sign of mourning. An older man and woman wearing hotel slippers, their faces gray, talk to a group of people. Slightly apart from them is a small, really young-looking woman, her feet covered in fuzzy socks, a large rip in the collar of her white blouse. Mrs. Wine takes her hand.

"I'm so sorry for your incredible loss," Mrs. Wine tells her. I realize with a pang that this is Mrs. Sandler. Her short, dark hair has a cool style, but it is greasy and her eyes are red-rimmed and swollen, with purple hollows underneath.

"This is my daughter and her friend. They were students of your husband's this year. He even got my Honey to pick up a book."

"I'm sorry," I whisper to Mrs. Sandler. I don't think she hears me. Behind her is a dressmaker's dummy stuck with pins, something shimmery draped over it, and next to that are bookshelves overflowing with books. It is easier to look at the dummy guarding the bookshelves than at her. On the bookshelf I can see a whole row of books with familiar spines. I start in surprise—it's the Most Likely To . . . series. Mr. Sandler said he was familiar with them, but I guess he must really like—have really liked—them too.

"Mr. Sandler was my favorite teacher," Honey says, and I pull my eyes away from the bookshelf. "But he especially loved Milla. She's really good at English." I try to give Honey a look, but she's focused on Mrs. Sandler and doesn't notice. "She's going to be in the speech contest next week."

"Raphi loved the speech contest," Mrs. Sandler says simply. "He loved his students." She smiles wanly at me.

"I'll make some meals for you and your kids when the shiva is over," Mrs. Wine says. Mrs. Sandler nods and looks toward three dark-haired little boys building a tower of blocks on the floor as shoes and boots tramp past them and around them. I hadn't even thought about Mr. Sandler being married. Or what his kids might be like. The middle boy looks just like him. There's so much I didn't know about Mr. Sandler, and now he's gone. I have a huge lump in my throat. The house is steaming from so many people, but I feel a chill inside me. Honey strides over to the three little kids, whose tower has just been accidentally knocked down by a teenage sneaker scurrying over it.

"Hey, I bet you have a great room. Can you show me?" She is crouching down to their little circle and speaking to the oldest, a boy about the same age as Max. Within a minute, she has one in a piggyback and two holding her hands, and they squeeze past the buzzing people toward the back of the house.

"Why don't I get you a cup of tea?" Mrs. Wine asks Mrs. Sandler, and Mrs. Sandler nods gratefully. "And I'll check your fridge and the meals schedule while I'm at it." Mrs. Wine gets up and heads toward the kitchen. I sit, rooted in my chair, by myself with Mrs. Sandler. My eyes keep finding the large tear in her blouse, like someone cut with scissors and then ripped the rest with their hands. Mrs. Sandler turns to me, her face brightening despite the hollows under her eyes.

"Are you the girl with the peeling-an-orange speech?"

I nod.

"Raphi thought it was hilarious—and smart."

"Honey also did oranges," I say quietly.

Mrs. Sandler cocks her head and then gives me another wan smile. "Yours was the one where how you do it reveals something about you, right?"

I nod again.

"Raphi told me about that speech—and that its writer was a bright student who had a lot to say." Mrs. Sandler's eyes are steady and sad as she looks directly at me. "Wouldn't you say he was talking about you?"

I don't know how to answer her, so I don't say anything. But I do know that I want to believe her.

On the way back home, it is dark inside Mrs. Wine's minivan, and I feel like the darkness is the sadness all around me.

If Mr. Sandler had never gotten into that fight with Rabbi Adler, maybe he would never have had a heart attack. If Rabbi Adler is thinking about that, he must feel very bad. My dad said a heart like Mr. Sandler's is a ticking time bomb, that when someone so young has a heart attack it's almost always fatal. Still.

"You never know how things are going to work out," Honey says, reading my thoughts. "You just have to do what you believe is right. Mr. Sandler did, but Rabbi Adler did too."

When Mr. Sandler left the first time, what I missed was that we didn't get to end things normally, like at the end of the year. Because how many teachers, even the ones I really liked, had I ever really seen again after we said goodbye on the last day of school? I *had* wanted him to see the light inside me. And to bring it out through my shell, like the osmosis of an egg white in the science project I was doing with Natalie. And then I'd wanted to visit him when I was older. If I'm honest, I only imagined that happening once—but once would have been enough for me to feel that he had stamped that light and fixed it in place where everyone could see it.

And after that it would have been enough to just know that he was out there. Probably in a classroom teaching other sixth-grade kids. But now there won't be that once. What Honey said yesterday on the massage table is right: What is so hard to process is the knowing for certain. We won't see Mr. Sandler again. I know it, but it still doesn't make any sense to me.

As I sit in the back with Honey—Honey, who went to play with the children when no one else thought to—a tidal wave of shame at my thoughtlessness and selfishness rises up and breaks over me. What Honey said about me in our fight might have been right too. Because I don't know about fate, destiny, and hashgachah pratit, but I suddenly see how I have been thinking only of myself. Like a movie screen unrolling down and showing images, I see Mrs. Sandler in her torn blouse and socks, and I see three little dark-haired boys, the middle one who looks just like Mr. Sandler—his dad. I see the shock, misery, and confusion on their faces. This family has broken, and the missing piece cannot be glued back in: It is gone forever. I take out Ezra's crumpled tissue from my pocket and wipe the tears flowing down my cheeks.

"Sometimes things just happen, Milla," Honey says, breaking into my thoughts again and handing me a clean tissue from a battered tissue box on the floor.

For a second, like the moon hovering in the darkness before a cloud covers it again, I have a picture in my mind of a red wheelbarrow, its surface wet and shiny. So much depends on everything else, and everything is connected. We just don't know why or how until it happens. And then we have to deal with it.

CHAPTER 17

RESULTS

The next week passes in a haze. On the morning of the speech contest, my class files down the hall and down the stairs, but when we get to the auditorium, they are shepherded into the rows of folding chairs while Ms. Silver puts her arm around my shoulder and leads me up a narrow staircase onto the stage. I swallow. My stomach feels like the huge food processor Mrs. Wine uses to make her potato kugel—it whirs and pulses, whirs and pulses, whirs and pulses.

All the stage lights are on and beaming toward an arrangement of folding chairs placed in a semicircle. Already seated is a girl I recognize from the eighth grade. Her hair is pulled back tautly under a thin hair band, her ankles crossed perfectly, her back straight, and a big smile on her face. Next to her is a boy I saw earlier this morning—his tie was loosened, cocky-like, but it is now straightened and tight to his collar. It was easy to identify the contestants because we are allowed to wear our own clothes today. I am wearing the black-and-white Shabbat dress that I carefully laid out last night on my chair, and the sequined cardigan I threw on top at the last minute this morning.

"Good luck!" Ms. Silver whispers to me, and gives me a gentle shove toward one of the chairs. The machine in my stomach churns.

"Milla! Milla!" I think I hear Max calling me. I hold my hand above my eyes like a visor and see him waving wildly from the front row, in a chair between my parents. My mom mimes a Wonder Woman "power pose," and my dad flashes me a smile and thumbs-up. The whole front row is reserved for the parents of the contestants, but my mother has the best seat, front and center. I see her take her phone out, ready to video me and send it to our whole family, all the pieces of my locket.

It feels hard to breathe.

My palms are clammy.

I try to cross my ankles like the girl in eighth grade. The machine in my stomach whirs and pulses.

The auditorium is a cacophony of kids from the middle school and fifth grade turning backward in their chairs, screaming in excitement to friends and siblings. I put my hand above my eyes again and peer into the audience. The partitions have been pulled back to make the auditorium as big as possible. I look for Mr. Sandler in his usual spot in the back corner, but of course he is not there. I catch a glimpse of Miriam sitting with all the fifth graders. I give a small wave. She looks behind her like I might be waving at someone else. There's no one behind her. She gives me a suspicious look and a half-hearted wave back.

"Milla!" I hear my name again above the racket and spot Honey, Natalie, Sophie, and Tali waving dramatically from a few rows in front of Miriam. "Whoop, whoop!" they shout, and raise their hands up like they're raising the roof. The machine running in my stomach slows down a bit. I smile and wave shyly, catching eyes with Honey. She hollers, "Go, Milla! You can do it!" I give her a thumbs-up, and she gives me a vigorous one back. I have been surprised to discover that all my angry feelings are gone, dissolved like the fog on the dashboard of my mother's car in the mornings. Me and Honey would've made up even if Mr. Sandler hadn't died. I wish he were here.

"May I have your attention, please!" Rabbi Adler says crisply from the podium. He taps the microphone. "Silence, silence, please. We are about to begin." The machine in my stomach picks up to a full-speed screech.

I sit up straight and edge forward so my feet will touch the floor. As Rabbi Adler quiets everyone down, I look at the contestants seated in a semicircle. To be fair, they look nervous too.

The boy with the tie is called first, and he flashes a smile at the rest of us before walking unsteadily to the front. I hear his voice, low and serious as he begins to talk about racism, but I can't seem to hold on to the words. I hear applause, and then it is the eighth-grade girl's turn and she glides like a ballerina to the front, where she talks in a musical voice about why she is a feminist. I check out my mother, who is listening carefully, her eyes glued to the girl. When she's finished, there is thunderous applause.

And then, suddenly, Rabbi Adler calls, "Milla Bloom."

It is my turn.

My legs feel like jelly as I walk to the microphone. I look for Mr. Sandler again, and of course he is still not there.

I close my eyes. I can hear my breath roaring in my ears. And then from far away I hear Mrs. Sandler's voice—*Wouldn't you say he was talking about you?* I swallow and open my eyes. The lights from the stage are making the sequins on my cardigan sparkle.

I take a deep breath and say into the microphone, "Ladies and gentlemen, rabbis, parents, and students—" My voice sounds a little wobbly, but also deeper and louder. I take another breath. Then I smile and hold up my orange. "How's everybody *peeling*?" I see the audience's amused expressions, laughter at their lips. They're with me!

Time slows down. All the bits I did in class are big hits here too—the Talmudic discussion getting an especially loud response from a section of Judaic Studies teachers sitting together.

I hardly even pause to register that I'm about to do the new part I've been practicing. "Take my mother, for example . . ." I say, smoothly going into a mischievous voice. "Who reveals much about herself in the simple act of how she peels an orange. Because in fact she despises the smell of orange peel on her fingers, and yet she loves my little brother *so* very much . . ." As I act out my mom peeling an orange with her latex gloves on, peeling it both carefully and disgustedly, laughter fills the whole auditorium and bounces back to me. I even see my mother laughing so hard she's leaning into my father. It feels like a light has come on inside me, warming me up. Making what is inside me glow so everyone can see. It is the best feeling in the world. As I get ready for the ending, I keep my gaze front and center, on my mother.

"And in conclusion, you may not have realized this before, but now you do: How you peel an orange says a lot about you. So"—I pause and smile mischievously again, my eyes now scanning the room, taking it all in—"orange you going to ask *me* how I'm peeling? Thank you."

I hear the audience's full-bodied howls and then crashing applause. There are whoops from the midsection of the room and shouts of "Mi-lla! Mi-lla!" My heart is racing, but the machine in my stomach has stopped its whirring. I somehow find my way back to my seat.

Time goes by in a daze. I watch contestants stand up, go to the podium, and then sit down.

Rabbi Adler is back at the podium. "And now we are going to ask the contestants for something extra this year," he says into the microphone. My head snaps to attention. What?

"Before the judges make their final decision, we would like each contestant to come up and tell the audience and judges why they think *their* speech deserves to win. Because words have power, and it's important to understand the power you wield with them."

The other contestants look as stricken as I feel, but the eighth-grade girl quickly shakes it off, and confidence returns to her face. She glides over to the microphone. "My speech on feminism is important and deserves to win because my mother was told to reach for the stars and that she could be anything she wanted to be—and yet I watch her constantly battling between motherhood and career. We've come a long way since *her* mother's time, but we still have much more work to do." I gulp. I see my mother's eyes rapt on her. And I see what must be her own mother wiping a tear from her eye.

"Milla Bloom," Rabbi Adler calls, summoning me back to the podium. I walk with leaden legs. There is a ringing in my ears.

"Um," I say, my voice sounding eerie now in the microphone. "Well—" I take a step back as the microphone screeches and everyone winces. I try to adjust myself to where I was before when I said my speech. Why *do* I think my speech deserves to win? Because it made people laugh. Because I worked hard on it. Because then I'll be a somebody for once. I mean, I know it's good—I wouldn't be here if it wasn't. I know the audience liked it—I could hear them genuinely laughing and genuinely listening. I take a deep breath and hold the microphone.

"I think my speech deserves to win because it was funny. And, well, people never realized before how much they tell other people about themselves from such a small act as the way they peel an orange."

This time there is awkward silence from the audience. I trudge back to my seat. I avoid looking at my mother.

After everyone has their turn, the judges, who are sitting at a folding table at the front of the audience, confer. They huddle together whispering, looking at their notes while Rabbi Adler leads the audience in a Jewish song. I feel like something sticky is on my skin. Orange juice that has dried.

Finally, one of the judges signals Rabbi Adler, and he shushes everyone again so he can announce the results.

"We had some very strong speeches this year . . . and some unusual ones." He smiles. I shift in my seat and try to keep my expression neutral even though it's obvious he's talking about mine. Why did I ever think I had a chance?

"It is my honor to award Samuel Mizrahi third place for 'Why Does Racism Still Exist?' An excellent question and one he did a wonderful job exploring. Well done, Samuel. Please come up to receive your award."

I mold my mouth into a smile as the boy with the tie now flashes us a huge grin and struts to Rabbi Adler. My face feels cold. I can't believe that somewhere deep in my heart I actually thought for a minute when I finished my speech that I had a chance at third.

"—and in second, with a most unusual and yet entertaining—and surprisingly perceptive—speech, we have Milla Bloom with 'How Are You Peeling?'"

What?

Did Rabbi Adler just call my name?

I hear a sound come out of my mother's mouth that sounds a lot like a whoop. I exchange a look of shock with her.

Oh my goodness!

Second place?!

Everyone is cheering. I float like a balloon to Rabbi Adler, receive a plaque, smile for cameras flashing, and drift back to my seat. Oh my goodness.

Ms. Silver rushes onto the stage from the wings

and hugs me. "This is the first time a sixth grader has placed so high!" she whispers.

I sit in shock, a warm light glowing from my stomach, the air around me like a soft cushion.

When it's all over and Kayla Levy, the eighth-grade girl with the hair band, has accepted her award for first place, I follow the rest of the contestants down the hidden stairs into the cacophony of the auditorium.

"Here's our star!" my dad says, greeting me with a bouquet of flowers. My mom hugs me, and Max jumps up and down and asks if he can hold my plaque.

My mom takes a step back and, holding my shoulders, says, "You should be so proud of yourself." Then she gathers me in her arms again, crushing the flowers.

"You were right about the isms," I shout over the noise in the auditorium.

"I'd rather I wasn't," she says.

"You're not mad I did you wearing your gloves?"

She laughs, shaking her head. "What can I say? You got me exactly right."

I laugh too and then I stop. "Mom, you knew they were going to ask that extra part about why we thought our speeches deserved to win." It's a statement, not a question.

She looks guilty. "I obviously couldn't *tell* you. But I did tell you to think about it."

"I thought you didn't think my speech was serious enough to win."

"Things are funny when there is truth in them, Milla—people laugh when they can recognize themselves. If you'd have asked me, I would have suggested you say that your speech deserved to win because it reveals universal emotional truths that teach people something about themselves."

Huh? My speech did that? Well, now that she mentions it, maybe it did. I think of my mother peeling all those oranges for Max with her latex gloves on. I wonder if she knows Max could probably peel an orange by himself now.

When I get on the bus home, Honey has saved me a seat.

"You totally should have won," she says, offering me a piece of gum.

I smile at her loyalty. "It wasn't as serious as the others," I say, shaking my head to both the gum and what she's saying.

"So what?" she says, putting the pack in her pocket. "Yours was the only one people were even listening to."

"Yeah, but I really flubbed that part at the end—when we had to talk about why we thought our speeches deserved to win."

"That was so unfair for him to put you on the spot like that and make that part important," she says indignantly.

"Yeah, but Kayla was really good with all of it," I say. "Her speech was amazing—*and* she knew just what to say at the end."

"Well, there's always next year," Honey says.

"Yeah," I say, slumping against the seat. I sigh. Even though I came in second, people kept stopping me in the halls and saying congratulations. Everyone seemed to know who I am. But still, an uncomfortable feeling has been building all afternoon.

"Do you think it's weird that I was funny when I'm still so sad about Mr. Sandler?" I ask Honey.

"Huh?" she says, starting to blow a bubble with her gum.

"Like, I was thinking about him before I did my speech. But instead of it making me sadder, I kind of tried to do the speech for him."

Honey rolls her eyes. Her bubble has gotten huge. She sucks her breath in, and it pops with a loud crack. "Are you kidding?" she says, like she's swiping away cobwebs. Or nahrishkeit. "He would be so proud."

"I guess," I say, feeling a bit better. I don't know why, but like osmosis again, all the good feelings from this morning have been trying to seep out.

"Milla, don't ruin something great you did with bad feelings. You're trying to take something big that you did and make it small."

"Yeah," I say, thinking how well Honey knows me. I take a deep breath. There is something I have been wondering about for a long time that I need to ask her. "Honey, did you let me win—in our class?"

Her eyes bug out, and she stops chewing her gum, her mouth hanging open. "Are you serious?" she says, raising her eyebrows and tossing her ponytail. "Milla—c'mon. How well do you know me? Would I *ever* purposely let anyone win?"

Hmmm. I *do* know her pretty well, and I realize she makes an excellent point.

She laughs, and then I laugh too.

It feels good.

Passover

CHAPTER 18

BITTER HERBS

When I come down for breakfast the morning of Passover eve, the kitchen has been transformed. Every surface is covered with heavy white plastic cloth, cut to the exact shape of the counters, blue electrical tape holding down the edges.

"Don't give me that face, Milla Ruth," my mother snaps when she directs me to where she's set up a supply of paper plates, plastic cutlery, and other environmentally unfriendly disposables on a covered folding table next to her workstation. "It's just for dairy meals, and it's just for the week."

"Okay," I say, holding up my hands defensively. Passover celebrates how God took the Jewish people out of Egypt, where they were slaves to Pharaoh. Because they escaped in such a hurry, there wasn't time to make their bread properly and let it rise, so for the eight days of Passover, we eat unleavened bread, which isn't bread at all; it's matzah. In fact, any type of grain is forbidden. The forbidden stuff is called chametz, and the house has to be scoured for any crumbs.

For the last two weeks, my parents have been wiping down every cabinet, closet, and corner. Boxes of food stamped KOSHER FOR PASSOVER, plus new dishes, cutlery, pots, pans, and utensils only to be used on Passover have been piling up in our laundry room.

"Where're Max and Dad?" I ask my mom as I pad over to the table. Max and I have been off school for Passover break since two days ago and my father has taken the week off work for the holiday, but the house has a hushed, empty feeling to it.

"I needed a little peace and quiet," my mom says, taking a thick white root-looking stick out of the fridge. "Dad took Max to run some last-minute errands so I can just motor through what I need to do still for tonight."

I nod. I know it's a lot of work to get everything ready for the ritual seder meals. "I'll help when I finish breakfast," I say, pouring some Passover "cereal" into a plastic bowl as a sinus-clearing smell overtakes my senses.

"Mom, what *is* that?" I ask, after trying to take a spoonful of cereal without breathing in.

"Horseradish for tonight," my mom says, vigorously running its edge back and forth over a grater.

Bleurgh, the smell of the bitter herb is sharp! I put my spoon down and push away my bowl.

"Oh good, you're done," my mom says. "Can you peel these eggs for me?" Like bitter herbs, an egg is one of the symbols on the seder plate, and my family serves one whole boiled egg in a small dish of salt water to everyone at the seder.

"Uh, okay," I say. When I lift the tea towel from the bowl my mother points to, I am met by the assault of fart smell. I make a face my mother can't see. Then I hold my breath, pick up an egg, crack it against the plastic-covered counter, and gingerly start peeling.

"Milla! Get a newspaper or paper towel," my mother says when she glances over at my progress. I look at the pile of shells on the counter.

"Oh, good idea," I say. I tear a piece of paper towel and try to scrape the shells onto it. They fall on the floor.

"Millaaaaaa!" my mom says.

"Sorry," I say, wincing. I tear another piece of towel and try to scoop up the shells with it.

"Milla Ruth, where's your common sense?!" my mom says with exasperation. "Broom, dustpan."

I tell myself she's on a short fuse because of all the

work to get ready for the holiday and just get the broom without saying anything. Afterward, I put a fresh paper towel down on the counter and gently tap another egg against the bowl. I work slowly, bits of shell sticking to my fingers, and try to breathe through my mouth as the stinky egg stench competes with the eye-watering smell of the horseradish.

"Can I turn on the radio, Mom?" I ask after a few minutes. "It's a little quiet."

"Please, no, Milla. I already have a headache." She blows at the strand of hair over her eyes.

"Okay," I say glumly, and we continue in silence except for the hum of the refrigerator. Passover is a holiday people usually spend with grandparents, cousins, uncles, and aunts—guests galore at the seders. Since I can remember, each year we've alternated between having Pesach with my mom's side of the family and my dad's, but since everyone is coming here for my bat mitzvah in six weeks, this year it's just us and Aunty Steph. Well, and Shmuel Yosef. And one special guest I invited for tomorrow night. But still. Honey sent me a picture of their dining room table all ready for the seder tonight—it's set for thirty!

When I'm done, I throw away the shells, find a

clean bowl for the peeled eggs, and wash my hands. "Okay, see you later," I say.

"Where are you going?" my mother says.

"To Honey's—I promised I'd help them." This isn't strictly true, but I've had enough of the smell and the quiet in here.

"Don't you think they have enough helpers?" my mother says saltily.

"The more the merrier," I call, already at the door.

When I get to the Wines', I ring the doorbell. No one answers. The knocker is still missing. But Mrs. Wine's minivan is in the driveway. I know they're all home.

As soon as I let myself in, I am enveloped in the intense smell of fish and something burning. The dining room doors have been thrown open, and the table has been extended out into the hallway, waiting for all the guests tonight. The kitchen, its counters covered in specially fitted boards, is empty.

"Hello?" I call. I look in the den. Aaron is there with Abbie, his therapist.

"Say hi to Milla, Aaron," she instructs, using her fingers to remind him about eye contact.

"Hi-Mil-la," he says. He raises his eyes for a

moment from the laminated flashcards on the table.

"Hi, Aaron," I say, smiling. Behind him through the window, I see Mr. Wine, Josh, Dan-Dan, and Micah standing around a fire in the backyard. They must be burning the chametz, which some people do the morning Passover starts. I think my dad and Max are taking ours to the dump.

"Sorry for not answering the door," Abbie apologizes. "The bell's been going nonstop this morning, and I can't keep interrupting my session with Aaron. They're all in the Passover kitchen," she explains, pointing to the floor.

I head down to the basement, the smell of fish getting stronger with each step. Most of the year, the Wines' Pesach kitchen sits behind a closed door off the Ping-Pong room and looks like any other closet door. But as I reach the bottom step, I see that the kitchen doors are wide open—and the Ping-Pong table is covered with a plastic cloth and serving as a temporary pantry of Passover tins and packets, bags of chips, candy, and boxes upon boxes of matzah. As I approach, I'm met with the source of the fish smell and the sound of singing.

Miriam is leaning against the doorjamb eating a

chocolate pudding. Honey, Ezra, Mrs. Wine, and Honey's bubbie are shoulder to shoulder in the tiny kitchen, in an assembly line making gefilte fish, shaping mini loaves of sweet ground fish and then dropping them in a massive pot of boiling water. Above the roar of the stove fan, which is vainly trying to suck out the fumes of the fish, they are singing rounds of "Ma Tovu"—"What Is Good?"—which makes me smile to myself in fondness. The Wines' voices are *not* good, but that never stops them.

"Hi," I say. Miriam takes a spoonful of pudding. The others keep singing, their backs to me. I feel like I am knocking on their heavy front door.

"Hi!" I shout as loud as I can.

"OH, HI, MILLA!" Honey says, turning around. Ezra glances over his shoulder and nods in greeting.

"Can I help?" I offer.

"WHAT?" Honey says.

"CAN I HELP?" I shout.

"SURE!" she says.

But as I try to move in from the doorway and squeeze myself into the kitchen, Miriam blocks my way.

"WHY AREN'T YOU HELPING AT YOUR OWN HOUSE, MILLA?"

I start in surprise. She's so rude, that Miriam! Just when I thought she was getting better. "Well—I *did*," I say. I think about my mother standing in our kitchen now by herself. The hum of the refrigerator. But that's what she said she wanted—peace and quiet! Then I wonder why when I am at the Wines', chipping in is fun, even if that happens to be peeling a five-pound bag of potatoes—or squeezing into a stinky kitchen to make fish balls. It doesn't feel like I am really even helping, more just that I am a part of something.

Honey hip-checks Miriam to get her to move over. "Ima!" Miriam cries, tattling.

Mrs. Wine stops singing and turns around.

"Milla, sweetie!" she shouts, giving me a smile as her fingers still work the fish. "I'm not kicking you out, but I'm kicking you out. We're fine here. Go home, and tell your mother she shouldn't make gefilte fish. I'll send some over right before the seder so she doesn't even have to worry about where to put it!"

Miriam lolls against the doorjamb and licks her spoon, a smug look on her face. "SEE, I TOLD YOU TO GO HOME TO YOUR OWN FAMILY." Everyone else's backs are to me, and they don't hear what she says. I gulp and try to breathe through the smell and heat of the kitchen. I hate Miriam.

"Okay, thanks, I'll tell her!" I call to Mrs. Wine's back.

"A Chag Kasher v'Sameach," she calls over her shoulder, wishing me a happy and kosher holiday.

"With shalom and re'us!"—peace and friendship—Honey's bubbie adds without turning around.

"AMEN!" says Mrs. Wine.

"Thanks," I say. "Um, so I guess I'll go home now." And when no one turns around again, I leave.

When I get back home, Aunty Steph is sitting on a stool by the island, staring at a Styrofoam hot cup in front of her. A fresh box of chamomile tea is beside it. She looks really upset.

"What's wrong?" I say. "Is it all the plastic and disposable stuff? Mom says it's only for dairy, that she can't deal otherwise, or buy two new sets of dishes."

Aunty Steph holds her arms out to me to give me a hug. I am enveloped in the end of the lavender smell and the beginning of very strong body odor.

"Um, are you okay?" I say. I pat her back and try to raise my head to look quizzically at my mother, who has just entered the kitchen carrying a large, heavy-looking box.

"Look what I found in the spare room," my mother says, putting the box down gingerly on the counter and lifting something out of it. It is covered in bubble wrap. "Dad's kos shel Eliyahu." She carefully unwraps the protective layers and holds up a beautiful colored-glass goblet, meant to be filled to the top with wine and put in the center of the Passover table for the prophet Elijah—Eliyahu—to come visit.

"Remember all our family seders, when Dad was alive?" my mom says to Aunty Steph. "You were so little, but you would insist on staying up for the whole thing. I used to take you by the hand, and we'd open the door for Eliyahu together." My mom sniffles a little. I forgot that she and Aunty Steph are always a little sad and miss my grandfather right before a holiday.

"Yeah," Aunty Steph says, and holds me tighter for a minute before letting go.

"You know, he didn't even tell me he was having doubts," Aunty Steph says quietly. "We could have talked about them. We could have worked through them."

I am confused. I don't think Aunty Steph is talking about my zaidy, who died when I was little.

"Shmuel Yosef isn't sure he wants to be religious anymore and told Aunty Steph last night that he will not be joining us at the seders," my mother clues me in, carefully carrying the goblet through to the dining room, where the table is now set for tonight.

"Maybe he wants to be with God, but he doesn't want to be with me," Aunty Steph says, sounding really down.

"Stephie," my mother says, coming back in to the kitchen and over to me and Aunty Steph. "You're better off without him. He's missing something, and he wasn't done finding it. He might never find it."

"But—" Aunty Steph says. "He didn't grow up in a nice home like ours. He didn't have a mother to raise him like we did."

I see my mother stiffen and pull away. "It's not your responsibility to take care of him, Steph. When you have children, trust me, there will be plenty to take care of. You don't need a partner to drag you down. You have so much more to offer than he does."

My own body stiffens. My mother did all this stuff just to have two kids, but she keeps saying things that make it sound like taking care of us is such a burden. I think about her snappishness these last few weeks and realize it's not just about Passover. All the sighs she thinks I don't hear and that conversation with my dad when Mr. Sandler left the first time. She said she left her job and career for us, and that she didn't feel like it was a choice. It was something she had to do. But . . . it doesn't feel like any of the stuff she's doing for us is making her all that happy most of the time. And now she's basically just admitted it: We drag her down.

Aunty Steph angrily slaps her hand down on the plastic-covered counter and accidentally upends the hot cup. I start in surprise and jump back as chamomile tea sloshes all over the counter and onto the floor.

"What he has to offer?" she yells, not crying anymore. "I love him! If he loves me back, that's what he has to offer. I know things haven't been easy for you, Lori, but you could get over yourself once in a while and look around. Not everything is about you." She gets off her stool and strides to the front of the house, slamming the door behind her.

Suddenly, there is silence again, and I realize my mouth is hanging open. I've never heard Aunty Steph raise her voice. I never considered she could tell off my mom. I kind of want to cheer for someone standing up to my mother for once, but the look on my mother's face right now stops me in my tracks. I wonder what Aunty Steph meant about things not having been easy for her. I wait to see if she's going to say anything, but my mother's mouth is clamped tight. She grabs a roll of paper towel, thrusts it to me without a word, and stomps out of the kitchen. I hear her footsteps on the stairs and then the slam of her bedroom door.

I mop up the tea as best as I can. I go to the dining room and remove the name card and place setting for Shmuel Yosef. Then I go upstairs to my own room and slam my own door. I try calling Honey, but the phone just rings and rings. They are probably still down in their Pesach kitchen singing. I am ashamed to admit it, but I'm so jealous it makes me sick.

When Passover starts, Aunty Steph does not sing "lai-la-lai" and sway with my mother. She stands like a statue while my mother lights the candles.

Usually, my father leads the seder, unless we are with my grandparents in Israel, and then my grandfather leads. But either way, normally we are so many people sitting around a huge table and everyone reads out loud together from the Haggadah, which tells the story of Passover. This year, we are just five people sitting at the end of our dining room table like it is any old Shabbat.

Aunty Steph, who always fills our ears with her pretty voice, doesn't join in a single song. My mother sits in stony silence. My dad, looking pale and waxy in the white kittel robe he wears to lead the Passover seder, sits at the head of the table reading from the Haggadah, but no one reads along with him this time. Max sits next to me, importantly flipping the pages of the Haggadah he made in school. "Is it my turn yet?" He keeps interrupting my dad. "I'm doing it myself this year, you know." Every year, me and Max sing the "Mah Nishtanah" together—or at least the first verse, which is all he knows. But it's really the job for the youngest child at the seder.

"I know," I keep telling him. "In a few minutes." I find it's all I have to say. I usually jump in whenever there is something I have learned in school about the part of the Haggadah we are up to, but like my mom and Aunty Steph, who both have brought copious handwritten notes and commentaries on the text but have so far not said a single dvar Torah, I don't feel like contributing tonight.

"Okay, Maxie, you're up," my dad says finally.

Max smiles and stands on his chair. He opens his mouth. Nothing comes out.

"Go on, Maxie-pie," my mom coaxes.

Still nothing comes out. A confused look crosses his face. He's forgotten the words.

"Mah nishtanah, ha-lailah hazeh," I prompt with the opening question, "Why is tonight different from all other nights?"

"I said I was doing it myself!"

"Okay, sorry," I say, but it's too late. His face has turned red, and he stamps his foot on his chair.

"Myself!" he shouts. Then his face crumples, and he bursts into tears, leaping off the chair and crawling underneath it, where he pulls himself into a ball and wails.

"I knew I should have napped him this afternoon if he was going to stay up tonight," my mother snaps, her tone of voice suggesting that she had thought it was a good idea but we had told her otherwise.

When it's finally time to wash and have matzah, Max refuses to come. I pass him a piece of matzah under his chair. But when he wants my mother to serve his chicken soup under the chair too, she hauls him out, scoops him up, kicking and screaming, and carries him up to bed. When she doesn't come back down after ten minutes, my dad goes to check on her. "They're both fast asleep in Max's bed," he reports with a sigh.

Me, my dad, and Aunty Steph carry on as best as we can. At one part of the seder, we invite all who are hungry to eat with us. But I can't imagine even some stranger wandering the street would be tempted to join our gathering. Outside, a storm starts, and every time the wind blows the branch of a tree against the window, Aunty Steph looks toward the door expectantly, until she realizes it was just the wind. My grandfather's Elijah cup, sparkling and filled with wine in the center of the table, remains untouched. Neither Shmuel Yosef nor Elijah have decided to join our seder. Who could blame them?

In school, everyone always brags about how long into the night their seders go. "We didn't finish until after one a.m.!" someone will say. "Ha! We were singing until two in the morning!" someone else will say back. This year, we are done by 10:30 p.m. I bet Honey's seder isn't even up to the meal yet. They are too busy belting out the Passover songs in a dozen different keys.

CHAPTER 19

MAH NISHTANAH...

When I wake up the next morning, the storm is gone and the sun is shining. I decide to put the bad feelings from last night aside. It's a new day, the first official day of Passover, and I can have matzah and butter for breakfast. I leap out of bed and pad downstairs, where my mother is carrying the dirty dessert plates from the seder into the kitchen.

"You're up early," she says.

"I'll help you clean up," I say.

"You can have breakfast first," she says.

"No, I want to help," I insist, thinking of Miriam and Honey and Mrs. Wine. I carefully lift the Elijah's cup from the table and walk toward the kitchen. My bare foot steps on something hard, and I stumble. "Ow!" I cry, picking a piece of Lego out of the ball of my foot and losing my balance. The Elijah's cup slides out of my hand and sails through the kitchen door.

There is a crash, and then the sound of hundreds of glass shards scattering across the tile floor, mimicking the sound of the rain pelting outside last night.

Then there is an absence of sound as my mother and I stare at each other in horror.

Aunty Steph rushes down the stairs, calling, "What just happened?" She stops when she sees. Max, who must have still been sleeping and didn't go to shul with my dad, follows behind her.

"Now Eliyahu will never visit us!" Max cries.

"I'm sorry," I say in a small voice.

"Okay, show's over. Everybody out. I need to clean up," my mother says tightly.

"Geez, Lori, do you always have to be such a martyr?" Aunty Steph says, and points to my mom's bare feet and then to her own rubber slides. "Let me clean up." She crunches over the glass to get to the broom.

I go to the door and grab my sneakers. "I'll help too," I say, tugging a shoe over my heel.

"You've *helped* enough, Milla," my mother says. "Just get out of here. Everyone. Just get OUT!"

Max turns with a yelp and runs up the stairs. I stand frozen in place.

"Oh, Lori," Aunty Steph says with disgust. "Honestly."

I look down at my shoes. I am standing by the door. A rage I have been trying to ignore that has been hovering since yesterday—or maybe a lot longer than that—rises up through my belly, fills my throat, and feels like it is coming out of my eyes. I'm so angry I suddenly can't see.

"You know what, *fine*," I shout. "I *will* get out. God forbid I should drag you down anymore!" Before I even know what I'm doing, I've opened the front door with trembling hands. "BYE!" I scream, and slam the door shut behind me.

I've marched down the driveway before I realize that I've left the house in my pajamas. Who cares? No way am I going back there.

I stomp toward the Wines' like my feet are on autopilot, my mom's voice bouncing around my head.

Milla Ruth, where's your common sense?

Milla Ruth, just say thank you.

Milla Ruth, don't give me that face.

This is my face, Mom, take it or leave it!

I tear down the path, my anger fueling my legs until I've reached the Wines' front steps. I leap up them two at a time. I knock.

No one answers.

I knock again, harder, flinching as my bare knuckles meet the heavy door. The empty holes where the knocker used to be mock me.

I bang with my fist, my breath coming ragged.

Still nothing.

They're probably still sleeping after their late-night seder. Well, that's fine—I'll just wake up Honey. I practically live here anyway. They won't mind if I let myself in. Honey will be happy to see me. They'll all be happy to see me. Mrs. Wine will make me matzah and butter, and Honey will make me a hot chocolate. We'll all sit in the kitchen together.

I step forward to punch in the code and catch a glimpse of myself reflected in the shiny gold-colored keypad. In it I am looming, my head widened, my chest heaving. I look like a—well, like a vilde chaya.

I decide to sit on the step and calm down a little.

I press my hot forehead against the cold metal railing and try to inhale and exhale.

I listen to the birds chirping their April song.

I hear a plane droning overhead.

Slowly my heart stops racing.

My legs on the cold cement step begin to numb.

I rub my arms. I am only wearing a T-shirt and

my fuzzy pants. The storm from last night has cleared and the sun is shining in a brilliant blue sky, but the Wines' porch is shaded and the air is still crisp. I have the thought that I am like the Children of Israel who left Egypt in a hurry. I smile to myself when I think that I didn't even have time to grab some matzah before running out of my house. I stand up, and taking another calming breath, I rap my knuckles on the door one more time.

Still no one answers. As I step forward to press the buttons for the code, I see my warped reflection in the keypad again. I pause, my finger in the air. I know the image is distorted—widened and wobbly—like a fun-house mirror. But I can see that it also tells the truth: I am in my pajamas about to let myself into somebody else's house.

Everything leaps sharply into focus.

I am not Honey's sister. Miriam is her sister.

Mrs. Wine is not my mother. My mother is my mother.

I am not a Wine. As much as I feel like part of their family, my name is Milla Bloom.

I step down from the landing of the Wines' front door and head home.

As I walk back through the shaded path, a figure enters from the other side, wearing a trench coat and a baseball hat.

"Milla!" my mother calls at the exact moment I clock that it's her. She runs toward me and I take a few steps toward her until we meet in the middle. Then we stop awkwardly. She moves forward to hug me, but I keep my arms by my sides. "Shmuel Yosef came back," she says. "Right after you left. He realized he'd made a mistake, and he didn't want to lose Aunty Steph. So he walked all the way from his apartment. You should see his blisters."

"Is *that* why you're here?" I say incredulously. I'm furious, even though somewhere in the back of my head I'm happy for Aunty Steph. "You came to tell me that Aunty Steph and Shmuel Yosef have made up from *their* fight?"

"Well, no," she admits.

I raise my eyebrows, waiting. My heart is thumping again.

"I came to find you because I realized . . ." She takes a deep breath. "I should not have let you leave like that in your pajamas—"

"Mom!" I shout. *"WHO CARES!"* My eyes are jumping out of my face, and I want to scream in frustration. *That's* what she thinks the problem is here?

"Milla—" She takes my hand in both of hers. "I came because I don't want to fight with you. If this is how things are now, how bad is it going to get when you're really a teenager?"

I yank my hand away. "I'm basically already a teenager, and you still want to be in charge of me."

"I am in charge of you. I'm your mother. When you're an adult, you'll be in charge of yourself. Right now you're still only eleven."

"I'll be twelve in six weeks!" I yell, stamping my foot. She's completely missing the point.

"Okay, *twelve*," she says, smiling.

"Mom!" I shout. "STOP LAUGHING AT ME! I may not be Honey, but give me a little credit—I can do things too!"

The smile slides off her face. "I'm not laughing at you—" she starts, but steam is coming out of my ears, and I need to let it out all the way.

"You're always trying to tell me what to do—assuming I'm going to mess everything up if I don't do it exactly how you say—"

"But, Milla—" my mother interrupts. "That's my job—to keep you from making mistakes if I can, things that I learned from myself—"

"Yeah, but sometimes I'm going to make mistakes," I interrupt her back. I think about Naomi Dayan's Succot talk. "That's part of growing up, Mom! And that's the thing—I'm not you and I'll never be you. I'll only be me, even if I don't know exactly who that is yet. And I wish you could be proud of me for once for something that has to do with me. Because it really feels like you only like it when I do something that reminds you of yourself." Even my ribs are pounding, and every hair on my arms is standing straight up as everything I've been feeling these last months comes up through my body and out into the path, like I've vomited a worm that's been eating my insides.

My mother is standing very still, watching me with an expression I can't read. Without realizing it, I've started crying, and I furiously swipe the tears away. My mother puts her arm on my shoulder. "I'm always proud of you, Milla," she says.

"Then why don't you ever say it?" I shout, shaking her off.

"Because you shouldn't need to please me or

anyone else in order to feel proud of yourself! If all you care about are people validating you all the time, you'll never have the confidence to really make something of yourself."

"Like you?" I say, thinking about all her certificates and awards piled up in the spare room. "Well, before you had us anyway."

As if I've touched a bruise, she takes a step back. But then she comes forward and takes my hand again. I let my hand hang limp, but I don't grab it away this time.

"I'm incredibly proud to be raising such amazing kids. You don't have to do anything special to make me proud of you, Milla. And no matter what, I love you."

I swallow.

"But—" she says, and takes a deep breath. "Well, you're right. I'm realizing that I do resent how certain things turned out—or didn't turn out." I stiffen and try to pull my hand away, but she holds on tightly. "I thought I could have it all, Milla: a big career and a big family. And I had the big career." She shrugs. "But, well, four or five children—that's not what God had in store for me." She pauses to take another breath, and her eyes are glistening. She means the cityscape of needles in her bathroom, Max born so premature, not being able to have more babies. I feel my own eyes fill again. But this time not with rage.

"But I *do* have a big family. I have you and Max," my mother says.

I try to stop them, but the tears release from my eyes.

My mother's eyes are closed now. "Milla, I don't resent you or think of you as a—a burden. I love doing things for you, Milla—and I hate that you don't know that. That I haven't told you that enough." She opens her eyes and fingers my hand, rubbing my knuckles. A tear is running down her cheek too.

"But—it's just hard to be the person in the family that's always doing things for people without those people saying thank you, or even just acknowledging the work and time that goes into it."

I stiffen again and swipe my cheeks roughly with the back of my hand.

Just when I thought we understood each other, she says something that shows how she still doesn't see my side. I heave air out of my nostrils.

I am about to say, "Mom, but I do say thank you.

It's just that it's always your way or the highway." But I hesitate. It feels like we are going in circles. Her nose is dripping, and she is crying really hard now. She definitely doesn't look like she thinks she's so perfect.

I try to think: *What would Honey do in this situation?* In my head, I see her body jut forward to stand up for herself. But—I also know how much Honey cares about her family. And respects them. I've never even really heard her argue with her mother. And I think, as I have so many times, about what she said about my mother. And about what Aginéni said about her mother.

And then I think, *This isn't about Honey. It is about ME.* And not about me in a selfish way, but in the kind of way that this is about me and my mother and not anybody else and their mother. And then I think that maybe my mother has some other things she needs to deal with that are actually about her, and not really about me and her.

I let out a softer sigh of air.

I do know that she loves me. And that when she tries to tell me what to do, it's probably not *just* that she thinks she's always right, but it's to protect me from one thing or another—especially pain. Even if I do need to go through some of these things to grow up and become myself. Even if I don't even really know exactly who that is yet.

And maybe . . . well . . . maybe I haven't acted as grateful as I could be for the things my mom does for me, or for what I have.

I bend my body forward so I can put my arms around my mother and I lean into her. Her trench coat feels funny against my cheek, but she holds me tightly and I hug her tightly back. We stay like that for a while.

"Oy, Milla, you're freezing," she says finally, rubbing my arms and then letting go to start taking off her trench coat. "Here, take my coat."

"No thanks," I say. "No offense."

She rolls her eyes. "None taken," she says with a rueful grin.

My mom and I walk along the path to our street. Just as we are coming up our driveway, she gives me a careful look.

"Milla, I know you often compare yourself to Honey, and that she's your matrix—" She pauses, looking like she wants to say more about that, but then shakes her head and puts her hands on my shoulders.

"Milla, I hope you know how happy I am that *you* are my daughter."

I think my mom means that for a long time I looked to Honey to design and build the house I wanted to live in. But instead of insisting that I try not to do that anymore, or that I offer plenty of creative input myself, I just blink. "Thanks, Mom," I say simply, suddenly realizing how much I needed to hear that. That I'm me: not Honey, or anybody else. And even though I know it's cheesy, I put my hands on her shoulders and say, "Mom, I hope you know I'm happy that *you're* my mother."

I expect her to roll her eyes at me and say something sarcastic, but instead she swallows and swipes a hand under her eye. "Thanks, Milla," she says, pulling me into a hug again. "I really needed to hear that."

As I hug her back, I realize I needed to hear myself say that too.

CHAPTER 20

... WHY IS THIS NIGHT DIFFERENT?

After I get back to my house with my mom, she and Aunty Steph lock themselves in the den for a while while Max and I give Shmuel Yosef breakfast in the kitchen; when they come out, they are both red-eyed and smiling. Later, as we light candles for the second night of Passover, we all sway and sing *"lai-la-lai"* with Aunty Steph as we make the blessing. I think how our voices sound pretty good together. My mom has a really nice voice too when she sings, and I notice she even has her eyes closed.

"Chag Sameach! Gut Yontuf!" my dad calls when he comes home from shul with Max and Shmuel Yosef.

"Gut Yontef!" Aginéni cries gustily from our living room sofa. Before candle lighting, Aunty Steph and Shmuel Yosef walked with me to her house and set up her new wheelchair on the driveway while I helped her down the front steps. Then we pushed her back to our house, her cane hooked onto the wheelchair handle—so that she could be my guest for our seder. My dad puts on his kittel, his cheeks ruddy tonight, while I haul Aginéni up and lead her to her seat at our dining room table, right next to mine.

This time we all read together, even Shmuel Yosef, who still stumbles over the Hebrew words he has only learned to read in the last year. We sing all the songs. Max stands on his chair, and I stand next to him, holding his hand while he asks the four questions perfectly, all by himself. I realize that last night I forgot to steal the afikomen from my dad, even though it is a tradition for the children at the seder to hold the special piece of matzah ransom, because the seder cannot continue after the meal until the afikomen is eaten for dessert. To be honest, it's one thing for breakfast with some nice salted butter, but who really wants dry cracker for *dessert*? Tonight I don't forget though. When my dad asks me what I want in exchange for returning the afikomen, I look over at Aunty Steph, who nods at me with encouragement.

"I want to change my bat mitzvah topic," I say. My mom looks at Aunty Steph in surprise. Aunty Steph now nods reassuringly at my mom.

"She's got a great idea, Lori."

"That she came up with herself," adds Aginéni

vehemently. My mother's face blanches—I guess Aginéni is still kind of scary if you don't know her like I do.

But then my mom squares her chin. "Can you pull it off in time?" she asks me and Aunty Steph. We both nod. "All right, then, do it," my mom says. She looks questioningly at my dad, and he nods. "We actually thought you were going to ask for something else, which we are still prepared to give you."

I look up in surprise.

"We thought you might like a new dress—a different one—for your bat mitzvah. I realize I pushed you into getting something you didn't want," my mom says, a guilty look on her face.

"Oh," I say. "Thank you!" I hesitate and then go for it: "Do you think I could get something made?"

"Actually, that's what we were thinking," my mom says, smiling at my dad. "That you might want to be involved. And I know a dressmaker who's just starting out with her own business and would be happy to make it for you for not a lot of money—it's good advertising for her."

"What about the peach dress?" I ask. I feel bad about the waste. And the money.

"There will be other bat and bar mitzvah parties. And after that maybe there's a local charity store that would be happy for a donation," she says, smiling. And that gives me another idea.

At the very end of the official seder, just before we get to the final songs, Shmuel Yosef holds up his hand.

"If you don't mind, I have an announcement," he says. "I'm going to Jerusalem to continue my Jewish studies." We all look at him politely. "And I've asked Steph if she will join me there. As my bride!"

"And I've said YES, he can be my groom!" Aunty Steph adds.

Aunty Steph and Shmuel Yosef are beaming and gazing into each other's eyes in the way that makes us all very uncomfortable. But instead of my mother making a funny face at my father behind their backs and mouthing "goo-goo eyes," my parents just look at each other and open their eyes wide.

"Mazal Tov!" my parents say at the same time. "Mazal Tov!" My mother takes my father's hand. And then I understand: Aunty Steph and Shmuel Yosef are engaged!

"MAZAL TOV!" I shout, congratulating them.

"MAZAL TOV!" I shout again, Max joining in with me.

"Oy, Mazal Tov! There's going to be a chaseneh," Aginéni says, meaning a wedding, and with pink spots in her cheeks. Who knew? Aginéni is a romantic!

I jump up to give Aunty Steph a hug. We probably hug a really long time, but I don't notice either way.

And then we all burst into my favorite Pesach song, "Chad Gadya," which is a list of things that add up kind of like consequences or chain reactions: A father buys a goat, a cat eats the goat that the father bought, a dog bites the cat that ate the goat that the father bought, and so on.

As we are singing, I think that it is kind of like life—the things we do affect other people and everything is related. It is kind of like the red wheelbarrow again too. But anyway, our singing sounds pretty good. Really good, actually. And even though we aren't that many people, for once my house is really loud. Good loud.

Before I put on my coat to walk Aginéni back home with my dad, I hand her brand-new copies of two books.

"*Most Likely To . . . Daisy* by R. S. Williams," she reads from the first cover.

"So you can reread it as many times as you like without having to return it to the library," I tell her. Her eyes twinkle with pleasure.

"And *Cashews* by Sylvia Lim," she reads from the second cover. "Nu, what's this one about?"

"It's kind of like 'Chad Gadya,'" I say. "I thought you might like it."

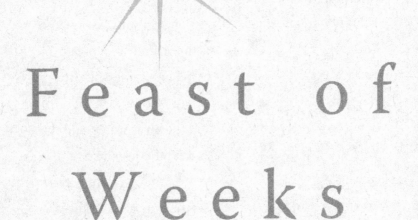

Feast of
Weeks

CHAPTER 21
FIRST FRUITS

After a long winter, everything is green again. All the neighborhood trees are flowering and perfuming the streets. My favorite are the lilacs. They always remind me of Shavuot, which celebrates when the Children of Israel received the Torah and began to rule themselves with their own laws. I guess it's fitting that this is when my bat mitzvah is too!

The Sunday after Shavuot, the air is warm and the sun shines late into the day as the guests arrive. We have a big tent in our backyard, and everyone walks around oohing and aahing at the blue and yellow colors my mom and I chose for the decor and exclaiming over the bite-sized delicacies passed around by waiters in bow ties. Mr. Rosen, the music teacher, plays Jewish music on his keyboard until it is time for everyone to find their seats, and my mother taps the microphone.

She welcomes everyone and says some thank-yous and some nice things about me and my journey toward adulthood. Then she pulls out a crumpled piece of paper and nods at me. I nod back.

"There's one final thing I want to share with you all about my daughter, Milla. I found this paper in our recycling bin last week after Milla cleaned out her schoolbag, and I felt compelled to rescue it. I don't know what the genesis or the context of it was besides something for Judaic Studies, but if you'll indulge me, I have Milla's permission to share it. If you want to know who my daughter is, her words speak for themselves:

"'How to Create a Kiddush Hashem'—a sanctification of God—'by Milla Bloom':

"'Who do I want to be in the real world? I want to be that person who might not win everything all the time, but who works really hard and deserves to win when she does. A person where the glass is half-full, even when things feel hard. A person who tries to understand what other people are going through. A person whose imagination can create exciting worlds for other people to dream in too and make other people laugh and sometimes cry, but the good kind of crying, the one that wrings you out and you feel much better afterward. A person who is pretty good at lots of things, not so good at some things, and who discovers something she's really good at and then gets to do it all the time and doesn't even feel like it's work because she loves it so much. A person who knows who she is and lets that guide her to make good decisions. I want to be a person who can make a Kiddush Hashem with these things that make me special.'

"My wish and bracha—my blessing—to you, Milla, is may you continue along your path; may your strengths continue to be channeled toward good; may any mistakes, setbacks, or unhappiness not be seen as roadblocks but simply the route anyone must take toward success and ultimate fulfillment, in whatever form that might look like for you. May you become the person you want to be, that you are already on your way toward, who *is* a Kiddush Hashem."

I go to my mom, and we hug for a long time, Aunty Steph–style.

Then Mr. Rosen breaks into a dancing song and everyone rushes out to the dance floor in two joyous circles, one for men and one for women. All my friends gather together and raise me on a chair. Then my parents' friends raise my mom and dad on chairs. Uncle Dougie and Uncle Robbie raise Max on a chair. Ollie and Oskie, wearing matching clip-on bow ties, stand on a chair together chanting "Up, up!" until finally Auntie Jacqui and Uncle Dougie grab one each and hoist them onto their shoulders, their hands clutching my aunt's and uncle's foreheads as they bop up and down to the music with glee.

All the pieces of my locket are here together in one place. I have a dance in the middle of the circle with my mom, and with Aunty Steph, and with the three of us, and with my bubbie, and with the four of us, and with Aunty Jacqui (and Oskie), and with the five (six) of us, and with my grandma, and with my grandma and Aunt Ronit and Aunt Ilana. I have a dance with Honey; and with Honey and Mrs. Wine; and with Aginéni, who I spin in her wheelchair; and with Tali and Sophie; and with Natalie; and with lots of other people and in lots of combinations. And what does this party say about me and my family? I have no idea. But I feel a warmth pervading everything, a brightness and light. I grab my mom, my dad, and Max and we dance in a circle, just us, while everyone here at this party to celebrate me and my family surrounds us whooping and clapping in time to the music.

When it is Honey's turn to give the best friend's speech, she stands in front of all the guests and says,

"Milla: You are thoughtful, observant of details other people wouldn't notice or think about, and introspective—which is a word you taught me. You know big words and use them without being a show-off. You are funny and have a unique style. I love laughing with you and just spending time with you. I feel lucky that we got to go to school together this year, and lucky that you're my best friend."

I rush to give her a hug, and I might be wrong— she might have had something in her eye—but I think she has to wipe her cheek. I find I have the same problem.

Then it is my turn to speak.

"Dear family and friends," I begin. The room is quiet, listening to me, and suddenly my stomach feels like Mrs. Wine's food processor again—whirring and pulsing. I smooth down my beautiful blue dress made by Mrs. Sandler and then finger Aginéni's butterfly brooch, which she has given to me as a bat mitzvah gift. She said I don't need it to make me more sparkly; it just shows on the outside what I'm feeling on the inside. I smile at her sitting at the table closest to where I am standing and then I smile out at the audience. "First of all, I would like to thank my Aunty

Steph, who no matter what was going on this year made time to learn with me at least once a week and worked on this speech with me."

Aunty Steph gives me a thumbs-up, and next to her is my mother, her face turned toward me expectantly. I smile again.

"The Sages say that naming a baby is a statement of her character, her specialness, and her path in life, and it's a most profound spiritual moment. The Midrash teaches us that there is one small area in which we are granted a glimpse of Divine wisdom. It comes to parents when they think hard to find the right name for their children.

"The names parents give their children are the result of a partnership between their effort and God's response. Some even say that an angel comes to the parents and whispers the Jewish name that the new baby will embody.

"The Hebrew word for soul is neshama. The middle two letters—'shin' and 'mem'—make the word 'shem,' Hebrew for 'name.' Your name is the key to your soul." I smooth my dress again and look down at all my friends, who have come to the front for the speeches, sitting cross-legged on the dance floor in front of me.

Out of the blur of faces, I register Honey, who is nodding and giving me two thumbs up. I nod back, silently appreciating how, in such small signals, Honey and I can acknowledge so many things all at once.

"My name is Milla," I continue. "And as everyone who goes to school with me knows, my Jewish name is Rut. And no offense to my parents, but the name Ruth, or Rut, never meant that much to me." There's a soft not-quite-laughter from the room at my admission. But my mother smiles ruefully from her table, and I beam an extra flash of gratitude her way: I've realized that my mom might not be very silly, but she's very good at seeing the funny side of things, even when it's about herself. I make a note to myself that maybe that's something I should try to do too.

"Nevertheless," I say, sending a special smile to my mom. "I was named Rut because I was born just before the holiday of Shavuot when the Book of Ruth is read. So when it came time to prepare for my bat mitzvah, my aunt and I decided to combine the two and study names as well as explore the significance of Ruth.

"Shavuot commemorates the acceptance of the Torah by the Jewish people, and the Book of Ruth describes the acceptance of the Torah by a single person, Ruth.

"As I become bat mitzvah now, I am no longer a child: The laws of the Torah are on my own shoulders, not my parents anymore. As I forge my identity in my journey toward being an adult, I too will make decisions about my beliefs and my commitment to my Judaism. And about who I am as a person."

I know my speech by heart, but I glance down at my notes, both for dramatic effect and also to steady myself before I go into this next part. "I've always worried a lot about what I have to offer—if like in the mitzvah of the lulav and etrog on Succot, I am like the willow—with no taste and smell. That I have nothing that makes me special."

I see my mother looking at me intently.

"I realized though that I do have taste and smell—and hopefully not bad ones." I smile at the appreciative laughter I knew to pause for. "But also I realized that my friends and family love me for who I am—my presence is important to them in and of itself." I smile again.

"There is one more thing I would like to say about names. Although Ruth is my Jewish name, in Hebrew,

Milla could mean 'word,' or it could mean 'mi lah,' 'who is for her?' Rabbi Hillel famously said in Pirkei Avot: 'im ein ani li, mi li?': 'If I am not for me, who will be for me? And when I am for myself alone, what am I? And if not now, when?'

"'Mi lah?' 'Who is for her?' I have to have self-confidence and independence as I mature. But if I am only looking out for myself, what kind of person am I?" I pause for another minute to search in the audience for Mrs. Kanin, the salesperson from What Goes Around. I found out that all of What Goes Around's merchandise is donated and the money the store makes from selling it goes to charity. So I've been volunteering there once a week for my mitzvah project. And even though Honey doesn't believe me, now that I've gotten to know Mrs. Kanin—who's a volunteer herself—I think she's actually pretty nice. She sees me catch her eye now and smiles back.

I suddenly realize I have almost come to the end of my speech. My stomach has been calm throughout, but it quickens again for a moment.

"Between being 'for yourself' and being 'for others' is a delicate balance," I say, gearing up for the finish but making sure I still say each word carefully and with kavanah—intention. "And when things need to be balanced, they often tip one way too much or the other too much until you figure it out. I have learned this year that mistakes are how you build yourself, how you find that balance, how you learn who you are, and what your values are."

"'If not now, when?' My journey to adulthood is long, but that doesn't mean I can sit back and wait for it to happen, that I cannot be the author of my own life. I need to make things happen that I want to happen, learn the things I want to learn, and be open to discovering new things about life and myself that I don't even know I want to know about yet. I am looking forward to it."

Then I smile, seeing all the faces of the audience as individuals again, my family and friends, my mother's radiance as she wipes tears from her eyes.

I am feeling very special—and very, very loved.

"Thank you for coming to my bat mitzvah."

CHAPTER 22

CLEANING HOUSE

After my bat mitzvah, some things change and some things don't. The first big thing that happens is that Aunty Steph and Shmuel Yosef leave for Israel. Shmuel Yosef is going to learn in a yeshiva, and Aunty Steph is going to "play it by ear." My mother just shakes her head and laughs. But we all cry when we say goodbye at the airport. Aunty Steph puts down her two huge hiking backpacks and gives my mom one of her longest hugs ever. And then she gives me an even longer one.

"Milla-babe, I can't wait to see your beautiful hair with flowers in it when you're a bridesmaid at my wedding!" she says, and then waves madly behind her as she tries to walk toward security wearing those two huge knapsacks, one on her front and one on her back.

"Why didn't she check those things?" my dad asks. But my mom just shrugs and laughs as she wipes her eyes again.

And speaking of my mom, something big happens

for her too. She announces that she is stepping down from her position as chairwoman of the board for my school. She says she will still be very involved but that it's someone else's turn to take the reins, and she is going to train to be an executive coach, which means she's going to help people "reach their potential." She and my dad are clearing out the spare room to make it into a home office so she can have somewhere quiet and private to study and work. I think this is probably going to be a really good thing for my mom, and I think her being happy will be better for our house, and our home. She's promised not to get rid of the massage table though!

On Shabbat afternoon, just before the last week of school, me and my mom are sitting in the den reading, Max playing with his Legos at our feet, when I notice the spine of my mother's book: *Most Likely To . . . Rion* by R. S. Williams, the first one in the series.

"Nice book," I say, smiling. She glances up.

"It's a real page-turner," she says, smiling back. "And the emotions feel so true. It reminds me how I felt at that age."

"I told you it was good," I say.

"You were right," she says, and I know her eyes are twinkling both because she is really liking the book and because of our secret discovery. When I had my dress fittings at Mrs. Sandler's house, I finally got up the nerve to ask her about the books.

"Jessie," I said, because Mrs. Sandler told me to call her that, and I do, because it somehow feels right, "I get that Mr. Sandler loved the Most Likely To . . . series as much as me, but how come you have so many copies of the same books? Was Mr. Sandler, like, a secret fan club lending library or something?"

I was joking of course, but to my surprise, Jessie got a shifty look on her face and hesitated.

"Something like that," she mumbled around a pin in her mouth. Then she glanced at the books and took the pin out from between her lips. "Okay, can I swear you to secrecy?"

I nodded. She looked at my mother. My mother nodded too.

"They're Raphi's books."

"Okay," I said. Of course they're his books; they're on his bookshelf. But my mother cocked her head.

"Jessie, are you saying . . . ?" my mother said.

"Yes." Jessie nodded, a little sparkle now in her tired eyes as she looked at me.

"What?" I said.

"Milla," Jessie said. "Those are Raphi's books. He *wrote* them."

My eyes widened in shock. He wrote them? Wait, Mr. Sandler . . . is R. S. Williams?

Jessie laughed, and my mother laughed too. I was too dumbfounded to do more than run over to their bookshelf, pull down one of the many Most Likely To . . . books, and stare at the front cover in wonder.

Mr. Sandler is R. S. Williams! He was writing young adult novels under a pen name. He was—is—the author of all those books. *My favorite books*. Mr. Sandler!

Sometimes since finding out, I am even sadder. It is another death, this one of my favorite author. I now know for certain that there won't be any more books in the series, or by R. S. Williams at all. But other times I am not exactly happy, but grateful, I guess, that at least I, and the world, got these ones.

On that day of the dress fitting though, Jessie gently took the book from my hand and opened it, flipping a few pages at the beginning until she came to what she was looking for. "Have you ever noticed how Raphi dedicated all these books?" she asked me, pointing to the words. They always say this—"

I read the words out loud: *"To my students—for inspiring me with their creativity and always pushing me to choose better.'"*

"I think he very much had students like you in mind when he wrote this," Jessie said.

And you know what? I have chosen to believe her.

I don't know though why Mr. Sandler chose to keep being an author a secret, never mind being the author of my favorite series. Sometimes I daydream that maybe one day he would have confided in me. But other times I think his dedications *were* his way of telling me—or at least telling me something even more important for me to hear.

Just as my mom and I are sitting at opposite ends of the couch in the den, smiling together over the shared memory of Jessie telling us about Mr. Sandler, there is a loud knock on the window. I jump up, startled, and then laugh when I see a swinging ponytail leaning way across the railing from the front steps.

"I was going to come over in a little while," I tell Honey when I open the door for her.

"That's okay," she says as we head back into the den. "I had to escape. My family is driving me nuts. I needed some peace and quiet!" We all laugh, but I suddenly wonder: Has she always been "escaping" her own house when she comes here? Is the quiet that sometimes makes it hard for me to breathe relaxing to her?

"You can escape to us anytime, Honey," my mom tells her.

"Thanks, Lori," she says, ruffling Max's hair and giving him a high five.

"Wanna have a Shabbos party now, Milla?" Max asks.

"Sure, Max," I say.

We gorge on cookies, gummy bears, and chips, and then play a round of Go Fish, which Honey creams me and Max at. When Max goes to shul with my dad for the evening prayers, Honey and I head upstairs to the spare room. It already has a big new desk against the wall and a new bedspread and pillows for the trundle bed to make it look more like a couch when no one's sleeping in it. The massage table is gone.

"Mom!" I cry, running downstairs to the den, where my mother is still reading on the couch. "You promised you wouldn't get rid of it!"

"And I keep my promises," my mom says mildly. "It's in the basement."

I make a face, and Honey and I trudge down to the basement, where indeed the massage table is set up against a wall near the old brown velour couch that used to be in my parents' first apartment before I was born. It's freezing down here, so I grab some tattered blankets from the closet where we keep old linens and camp stuff, and Honey settles herself on the massage table while I curl up on the couch.

"Do you ever wonder what kind of grown-ups we'll be?" she asks.

I realize I have, even though I have never put it into those words before.

I think about Mrs. Wine. I love her big personality, the way she loves gathering people around her and making everything a party. I love her house, and I love the home she has made in it. But I suddenly realize that I probably won't be like her when I grow up. I think I want children, but it is hard to think about that right now. I think I want to get married, but it is hard to think about boys as husbands. (Although Natalie says Noam likes me and is going to ask me to "go around," which is kind of like "going out" but not exactly because we're only twelve. And if he asks me, I will probably say yes.) I wonder if Honey will be like Mrs. Wine, and somehow, I don't think so.

Well, we each have our own destinies, but I like to believe our lives will also be about the choices we make for ourselves. I don't know that I'll be like my mother either. We've had some rough spots, and maybe I was angry at her. And then she'd be angry with me. And one thing follows another and affects another. I think I'm going to start calling it the "Red Wheelbarrow Effect." Or maybe the "Chad Gadya Effect." As I sit on the couch and look at Honey lying quietly on the massage table and staring at the low ceiling, chairs scraping in the kitchen above us, the overhead spotlights warm-toned and glowing on her skin, all I know for sure is I hope that, wherever I am, Honey will always be my friend.

"Maybe our kids will be best friends too," Honey says, turning to me. Then we both smile and raise our eyebrows at each other.

"I have a confession to make," she says.

"Okay," I say.

"Remember that time Miriam got a black eye from Gershi Plotzker's bar mitzvah?"

"Sure," I say. "It was Chanukah. We went up to the ladies' section to throw candy."

"Yeah," she says with a pained expression. "Um, so it was me who gave her that black eye. She was standing right by the bima, and I pelted her with a bag of candy. On purpose," she adds.

I just stare at her in shock. Then I feel the corners of my mouth tugging into laughter. But Honey looks really upset, so I try to tug them straight again and say, as neutrally as possible, "You have very good aim."

"Yeah, well, I didn't mean to give her a black eye. But I did mean to hit her."

"You could apologize?" I suggest.

"Maybe before Yom Kippur," Honey says. Her face has cleared, like some of the weight on her chest has released by telling me.

"My turn," I say, getting up and nudging her off the massage table.

This setup in the basement still needs some work, but it has potential.

Just before the end of school, all the girls in our grade do a bat mitzvah presentation. Mostly we just sing songs, but each of us gets a few lines to say too. The school hires Naomi Dayan to prepare us, and she tells me I am a "natural" at public speaking, but I make sure to watch her carefully and take some good tips from her anyway.

On the last day, Honey wins for community service points and gets a prize for math. I don't win anything, but to my surprise, there is a handwritten note in my report card:

Dear Milla, you were a pleasure to have in my class. When I spoke with Mr. Sandler before I had originally agreed to take his place back in December, he mentioned keeping an eye out for you as a kindred English spirit and he was right. Your comments were always on target and thought-provoking and raised the level of our discussions. Keep reading and keep imagining! Looking forward to next year.

Fondly,

Emma Silver

I know my mom says I shouldn't always need outside approval to feel proud of myself. But I've also learned that in relationships a little acknowledgment of everyone appreciating each other goes a long way.

After I read Ms. Silver's note through a few times, I fold it carefully and tuck it into the box Max's Lego airplane came in, where I've been saving things that are really important to me.

The day before I leave for sleepaway camp, I spend the afternoon playing with Max. Two huge duffel bags I packed with my mom are already in the trunk of her car, ready for us to take to the bus in the morning, and my knapsack is open by my bed, ready to throw in any last-minute things. I take down my bin of dolls, and Max and I give them names and story lines. He goes to get some of his own figurines to give us more variety and characters. The dolls and figures go on a trip to Miami in the Lego airplane. Two little figures we call Ollie and Oskie are the flight attendants, offering the passengers beverages that they dump on their heads and say, "All keen now!"

I show Max my apron fabric, which is still in the basket. "Maybe I'll use this to make airline uniforms the next time we do this," I tell him.

"You could do that?" he says.

"Sure," I say.

"Wow," he says, and throws his arms around me in a fierce hug.

"I'll do it when I get back from camp," I promise, giving him a tight squeeze back.

Then his friend's mom comes to pick up Max for a playdate, and my mom is in her office studying and all I can hear is the buzz of the air conditioners, so I grab something from our utility drawer and run over to the Wines'.

When I get there, Honey is on the front porch working a screwdriver into the door.

"Great minds think alike." I grin.

"Yup," she agrees, even though she doesn't know what I'm talking about. She steps back to admire her handiwork. The door knocker is now back on the door. It is slightly lopsided but looks secure.

"Nice job," I say.

"Well, enough was enough," she says, hands on her hips. "Someone had to do it, and like usual, that some-one is me." She grins. "And I'm avoiding packing." She raises her eyebrows, and I raise my mine right back.

"Fine, I'll help you," I grant with pretend-grudging generosity.

"It's just the Shabbos outfits and what goes with what that I hate doing, everything else is done," she says.

"Okay, don't worry," I say. "But first we need to take care of something else." I look at her screwdriver and the now-anchored door knocker. "Is the lady with the balloons still broken?"

"Is this the Wine family you're talking about?" she laughs. "What do you think?"

I take that as a yes, which is what I was pretty sure the answer would be considering I check on the china cabinet every time I am over. Mrs. Wine says that stuff is just stuff, but that sometimes it is also the ties that form who we are. I have realized that it is good to have choices, and the freedom to make them. But not everybody is so lucky to also have connections—visible and invisible—to family, to friends, to faith, that give us an anchor even as we explore the vast ocean of possibilities in the journey to becoming ourselves. So I am doing this for Mrs. Wine, and for Daisy, and also for myself. I pull the super glue out of my pocket.

"How about an art project?" I say.

Honey laughs, and I laugh.

And then, with our arms around each other, we go into the house.

AUTHOR'S NOTE

Some years ago, I heard a British Filipino author speak about growing up in the Philippines and reading mostly UK and US exports. She'd come to the conclusion that Filipinos weren't "allowed" in books. Hearing that sparked something in me I'd not thought about in quite that way until she'd said it. I realized that as a child growing up in a Modern Orthodox Jewish community in North America, I had internalized a similar sense of who and what *belonged* in books.

The closest I came to seeing something vaguely familiar to my observant Jewish home was in the All-of-a-Kind Family series by Sydney Taylor, which takes place in the early 1900s, and as I got older, in the adult novels of Chaim Potok, set pre– and post–World War II. But mostly, the only religious Jews I saw were in the Holocaust books I read over and over again—about hidden children, ghetto children, their way of life decimated, their families murdered. Although I am the granddaughter of four Holocaust survivors, thankfully my life in 1980s Toronto could not have been more different. I strongly support the need for children's Holocaust literature, and these books were a personal key to me understanding what my grandparents had gone through but never spoke about. At the same time, looking back, I see how hard it was to read over and over again about my people being victimized. Even today, the vast majority of mainstream books featuring religious Jews show them in the past, or as victims of persecution.

When I first started writing stories for children, the psychological impact of not seeing myself reflected back in literature revealed itself. In my first efforts, I copied the way other authors wrote: I sent my characters to regular public schools, not a Jewish day school; I had them dress up for Halloween, not Purim. In essence, I believed the world I knew best wasn't legitimate enough to write about.

It wasn't until I began to read my eldest child some of my own childhood favorites—*Ballet Shoes*, *Anne of Green Gables*, tons of Judy Blume, all the Ramona books, and *All-of-a-Kind Family*—as well as some new ones I was just discovering, like *The Penderwicks*, that I felt a shift inside me. I wondered if I could do what these writers all do so beautifully—show the importance and magnitude of small dramas in everyday life—but with contemporary Jewish characters.

That was when I began to write *Honey and Me*. While the story is about a world I come from and know well, it is not about me. Even Milla and Honey's peeling-an-orange speeches—which friends I grew up with will recognize as the topic I chose for our sixth-grade speech contest (a topic I myself borrowed from my older neighbor, and for which I even won second place)—were not my speech (at least I don't think so, I can't remember it at all!). But like Milla, it *was* the first time I felt like my creative interior world might be something interesting, even appreciated, in the outside world. When my fingers first typed a conversation between Honey and Milla, I not only felt them come alive on the page, I suddenly understood that you don't have to turn your back on who you are and where you come from in order to do something legitimate. Who you are—which includes your interior self and the external world you come from—can give you something very rich to share.

To me, the biggest mark of success for *Honey and Me* will be if readers love the particulars of Milla and Honey's life, friendship, and escapades—and also find in it something universal, in which they see themselves, whatever kind of home or community they come from.

My youngest child is now almost at the age where she can read my old favorites to herself, as well as discover new ones. I hope and wish for her and her siblings, and for all children, that they grow up seeing their lives reflected back, and also find themselves in lives completely different from their own.

GLOSSARY

In *Honey and Me*, Milla and Honey don't speak Yiddish (nor fluent native Hebrew), but below are words, terms, and phrases that are part of their everyday world and spoken language.

H = Hebrew
Y = Yiddish

abba (H)—dad
Adar (H)—the sixth month on the Jewish calendar
afikomen (H)—a piece of matzah hidden by children at the Passover seder
alte kaker (Y)—an old fogey
Amidah (H)—also known as the Shemonah Esrei, a silent prayer said standing
ani (H)—me/I
b'vakashah (H)—please
bar mitzvah (H)—coming of age at thirteen for a Jewish boy
Baruch Dayan ha'Emet (H)—Blessed is the True Judge; said upon hearing someone has died
baruch Hashem (H)—thank God, blessed is God
bat (bas) mitzvah (H)—coming of age at twelve for a Jewish girl
bat (bas) Torah (H)—a girl who observes Jewish laws and traditions
beseder (H)—okay, fine, all right
bima (H)—the table from which the Torah scroll is read during the synagogue service
bocher (Y)—an unmarried (usually young) man
bubbie (Y)—grandma

"Chad Gadya" (Aramaic)—a song about a goat sung at the end of the Passover seder

Chag Kasher v'Sameach (H)—Happy and Kosher Holiday; said on Passover

challah (H)—a bread loaf, often braided, eaten on Shabbat and festivals

chametz (H)—leavened grains, the consumption of which is forbidden in any form on Passover

chaseneh (Y)—wedding

chazerai (Y)—junk

chesed (H)—a primary Jewish ethical virtue; usually translated as "loving-kindness"

chevra kadisha (H)—Jewish burial volunteer committee

Chumash (H)—the five books of the Torah printed in book form (rather than a scroll for prayer service)

chutzpadik (Y)—cheeky, brazen

devorah/Devorah (H)—bee/the Hebrew name for Deborah

dvash (H)—honey

eire kichel (Y)—a light, sweet, and crunchy dough puff

etrog (H)—a citron fruit used with the lulav during the holiday of Succot

farbissineh (Y)—a sourpuss

farkakteh (Y)—lousy, messed up, ridiculous

gefilte fish (Y)—a ground fish loaf or patties traditionally eaten as an appetizer on Shabbat and festivals

Giveret (H)—Mrs.

gragger (Y)—noisemaker used on Purim

Gut/Good Shabbos (Y)—Good Sabbath

Gut Yontef (Y)—Good Festival, Happy Holiday

Gut Yor (Y)—Good Year, Happy New Year; said at Rosh Hashanah

Hagaddah (H)—the book of prayers, blessings, rituals, fables, and songs recited at the Passover seder

Hakadosh Baruch Hu (H)—another word for God

hamantaschen (Y)—triangle-shaped cookies with sweet filling, eaten on Purim

Hamotzi (H)—the blessing made before eating bread

Hamotzi lechem min ha'aretz (H)—the blessing over bread thanking God, "who brings forth bread from the earth"

Hashem (H)—God

hashgachah pratit/s (H)—Divine providence

"Hava Nagila" (H)—a Jewish folk song traditionally played at celebrations and danced to in a circle using the grapevine step

House of Hillel/House of Shammai—two rival rabbinic schools of Jewish law active during the first century BCE and first century CE named after their founders, Hillel the Elder and Shammai; the Talmud records hundreds of differences of opinion between Beit Hillel (the House of Hillel) and Beit Shammai (the House of Shammai)

Im ein ani li, mi li (H)—a famous adage by Hillel the Elder found in Ethics of Our Fathers: "If I am not for myself, who will be for me?" (". . . And when I am for myself alone, what am I? And if not now, then when?")

ima (H)—mom

Ivrit (H)—the Hebrew language

kavanah (H)—intention

kiddush (H)—the blessing over the wine on Shabbat; also a buffet after synagogue services

Kiddush Hashem (H)—sanctification of God

kittel (Y)—a white linen or cotton robe traditionally worn by men on Yom Kippur, when leading the Passover seder, and by a groom at a wedding

kos shel Eliyahu (H)—a goblet used at the Passover seder for Elijah the Prophet

kosher—food that complies with Jewish dietary law

kugel (Y)—traditional pudding (usually savory) eaten on Shabbat and Jewish festivals

kvetch (Y)—to complain

lashon harah (H)—literally "evil tongue"—speaking ill of someone

lein (Y)—to chant in a special tune from the Torah or megillah

lulav (H)—a palm branch used with the etrog during the holiday of Succot

"Ma Tovu" (H)—a Jewish song from the daily prayers; begins with the words "what is good?"

"Mah Nishtanah" (H)—the Four Questions asked at the Passover seder by the children

matzah (H)—unleavened bread eaten on Passover

megillah (H)—a scroll

Megillat (Megillas) Esther (H)—the Book of Esther, read twice on the holiday of Purim

Megillat Rut (H)—the Book of Ruth, read on the holiday of Shavuot

menachem avel (H)—the Jewish tradition of visiting a mourner to offer comfort and condolence

minyan (H)—a quorum of ten for communal prayer service

mitzvah (plural: mitzvot) (H)—good deed(s)

morah (H)—teacher

nahrishkeit (Y)—foolishness

neshama (H)—soul

netilat yadayim (H)—the blessing over washing hands before eating bread

nu (Y)—so, well

parsha (H)—the weekly Torah portion read in synagogue each Shabbat

partnership minyan—a prayer group committed to including women in ritual leadership roles to the fullest extent possible within the boundaries of Jewish Law

Pirkei Avot (H)—Ethics of Our Fathers, a Jewish text of ethical principles

re'us/t (H)—friendship

rugeleh (plural: rugelech) (Y)—traditional Jewish yeast pastry usually rolled with chocolate or cinnamon

seder (H)—the ritual Passover meal

Shabbat/Shabbos (H)—the Sabbath, which begins an hour before sundown on Friday evening and ends on Saturday night

Shabbat Shalom (H)—Good Sabbath

shalom (H)—peace (also means "hello")

"Shalom Aleichem" (H)—a song to welcome the Sabbath; "peace be unto you"

shamayim (H)—sky, heaven

Shanah Tovah (H)—Good Year, Happy New Year; said at Rosh Hashanah

sheitel (Y)—a wig covering a married woman's hair for religious purposes

shidduch (H)—a match between a couple for marriage

shiva (H)—the seven days of mourning following the death of one's next of kin; people visit mourners to offer comfort

shnorrer (Y)—grubby, moocher, a sponger

shofar (H)—a ram's horn symbolizing the High Holidays (Rosh Hashanah and Yom Kippur)

shul (Y)—synagogue

siddur (H)—prayer book

simcha (H)—happiness; used to mean a celebration

succah (H)—an outdoor hut in which meals are eaten during the festival of Succot

Talmud (H)—a compilation of rabbinic teachings and debates that serve as a "companion guide" to the Torah

tzadeikes/t (H)—female saint

tznius/t (H)—modest

v'nahafoch hu (H)—from the Book of Esther, used to mean "the tables were turned" vilde chaya (Y)—a wild, rambunctious person

yarmulke (Y)—kippa; skullcap worn by Jewish males

yeshiva (H)—a Jewish school where Judaic Studies comprise a significant portion of the curriculum; also a seminary for advanced scholars and rabbinic studies

Yiddishe neshama (Y)—Jewish soul

Yom hashishi (H)—the beginning of the Shabbat blessing over the wine on Friday evening

zaidy (Y)—grandpa

The Jewish festivals and holidays (in chronological order of the Jewish calendar, which starts in early fall):

Rosh Hashanah—The Jewish New Year. People pray and reflect, symbolized by the blowing of the shofar (a ram's horn) in synagogue, and rejoice in the new year, symbolized by ceremonial foods such as apples dipped in honey. The two days of Rosh Hashanah usher in the Ten Days of Repentance, also known as the Days of Awe, which culminate in the major fast day of Yom Kippur. Together, Rosh Hashanah and Yom Kippur are the holiest days of the year and are known as the High Holidays.

Yom Kippur—Day of Atonement, the most solemn day of the year, during which Jewish people refrain from eating or drinking for twenty-five hours and pray for forgiveness.

Succot—A harvest festival, begun five days after Yom Kippur. The holiday is named for the booths or huts ("succah" in Hebrew) in which Jews are supposed to dwell during this week-long celebration. It commemorates the temporary huts in which the Israelites dwelled during their forty years of wandering in the desert after escaping slavery in Egypt. Other symbols include the lulav and etrog.

Chanukah—The Jewish festival of lights, celebrated for eight days, usually in late November or December. Jewish people place a chanukiah (a nine-branched candelabra, or menorah) in their window. Each night an additional candle is lit to commemorate the miraculous avoidance of a massacre and rededication of the holy Temple in Jerusalem in the second century BCE. It is customary to eat foods fried in oil such as latkes (potato pancakes) or sufganiyot (jelly doughnuts), play dreidel, and give children small gifts.

Purim—A joyous holiday, usually occurring in late February or March, that celebrates a miracle that took place in ancient Persia when a plan to annihilate the Jewish people was thwarted. Jewish people dress up in costumes, give money to the poor, exchange gift baskets with hamantaschen (triangle-shaped cookies), and feast on food and wine. Megillat Esther (the Book of Esther) is read twice.

Pesach—Passover, an early springtime holiday that commemorates God's emancipation of the Israelites from slavery in ancient Egypt. Pesach is observed by refraining from eating bread and other leavened grains, since the Israelites fled before their bread could rise. It is highlighted by the ritual seder meals that include drinking four cups of wine, eating matzah and bitter herbs, and retelling the story of the Exodus.

Shavuot—Shavuot (also known as Feast of Weeks or Pentecost) celebrates the spring harvest and the giving of the Torah on Mount Sinai seven weeks after Passover. Symbols of the two-day festival include flowers and eating dairy foods. Megillat Rut (the Book of Ruth) is read in synagogue.

Note on Hebrew words that end with the "t" sound but sometimes might be pronounced with an "s" (e.g., bas mitzvah vs. bat mitzvah): This is a regionalism—the "s" sound is an Ashkenazi pronunciation for certain circumstances of the Hebrew letter tav— however modern Hebrew uses the "t" sound after the Sephardic pronunciation, and this has become the more common pronunciation. People from certain backgrounds (e.g., Mrs. Wine) might use the "s" sound; and for certain words (e.g., Shabbat/Shabbos), the "s" and "t" versions are both common and used interchangeably.

ACKNOWLEDGMENTS

Undying thanks and gratitude to Ben Gartenberg, for painstakingly coaxing this book into shape, for steadfastly pointing out my blind spots, and for having good reason and good instinct behind every note and edit.

Tracy Mack, for loving Milla and Honey and understanding what I was trying to do with their story. For seeing the through-line, for sensitive and organic edits that truly cut the "fat from the meat," for online shopping with me for Milla and Honey, and for making my dream of being an author come true.

Kait Feldmann, for loving Milla and Honey from the get-go and being my first publishing supporter. Leslie Owusu, for her enthusiasm and good cheer in shepherding *Honey and Me* through its exciting final stages.

Marijka Kostiw, for the clever and most perfect jacket design. Shamar Knight-Justice, for the most beautiful cover illustration: I had no idea what to expect, and yet when I saw the final version, it was as if Milla and Honey had flown straight from my brain and onto a book cover. I am still stunned every time I look at it.

Jackie Hornberger, Maddy Newquist, Jessica White, and Lisa Liu for expert copyediting and proofreading and for whose careful attention to detail I am so grateful.

Molly Ker Hawn, for her fierce and unwavering advocacy. For her good sense and sanity. For making me feel legitimate. And for seeing me through a very long journey with humor, empathy, and straight talking.

Hillel Drazin and Rabbi Mendy Maierovitz, for their help on the glossary—any mistakes are my own.

Yardaena Osband, for her sensitive and knowledgeable read on Modern Orthodoxy and my first proper audience. Lyn Miller-Lachmann, for her sensitive and constructive read on autism and for pointing out a missed connection that of course made perfect sense.

Rabbi Lord Jonathan Sacks zt"l, for the idea of Succot being a festival of insecurity (rabbisacks.org/archive/festival-insecurity-message -succot). Rabbi Benjamin Blech, for the ideas in Milla's speech about the significance of Jewish names (aish.com/judaism-the-power-of-names).

My husband, Hillel, a true "patron of the arts." And who thinks that says it all. I'll add, amongst many other things, for being my partner, making whatever I need to do work, being a reader, and being the father of our own "big family."

My daughter Niva, for the inspiration of Milla's words about being a Kiddush Hashem, and the original reason I started reading middle grade books again, and thought perhaps I could write my own. All my kids, Niva, Shai, Izzy, and Emmanuelle, who fill our house with laughter (usually, at least when they're not driving me bananas), busyness, and are the main characters in the sitcom that is our life and home. I love reading with each of you, along with everything else. Thank you for patiently telling your friends that your mom is an author whose book is coming out "soon."

Jacquie Hann, for seeing the writer in me and the salons in your home. Maggie Lehrman, who first saw the potential of *Honey and Me* as a real book and encouraged me to make Milla and Honey get into a fight. Elizabeth Law, for a crucial critical read of *Honey and Me*, as well as pivotal advice, help, and encouragement.

Miriam Craig, for being my first real writing friend; Peter Bunzl, for giving me writing and author advice; and Gail Doggett, for sound editorial feedback; and each of them for our endless conversations about writing and life. And to my wonderful writing group: Peter Bunzl, Miriam Craig, Gail Doggett, Tania Tay, Allison Friebertshauser, and Lorraine Gregory, for support during the bad times and celebration of the good, as well as karaoke, bowling, online party games, and lots of laughs. We started as a critique group and writing friends, but of course we've become so much more.

Thank you to SCBWI-British Isles for community and opportunities; and SCBWI in general for how I learned and continue to learn about publishing and writing.

The Association of Jewish Libraries and the Sydney Taylor Manuscript Award committee, for choosing *Honey and Me* for the Sydney Taylor Manuscript Award, and to Aileen Grossberg for "the call" and for being so lovely with all the arrangements as well as to Ralph Taylor for setting up the award and Jo Taylor Marshall for continuing to sponsor this award that encourages aspiring authors of Jewish children's books. The Harold Grinspoon Foundation, for sponsoring TENT: Children's Literature, of which I had the good fortune to be a fellow in 2019. *From the Mixed-Up Files ... of Middle-Grade Authors* blog (fromthemixedupfiles.com), for giving me a home to share my ideas about writing and middle grade books.

Stephanie Keiser, Sandy Steiner, and Sherri Libin, for being my oldest dearest friends. Sophia Steiner, for talking books with me. Audey Stanleigh z"l, who always believed in me: I miss you and wish you could see this.

And as this is a book about friendship, all my friends—thankfully, too many to name—you know who you are and I am so grateful to you for all our phone calls, walks, meals, time spent together, confidences, and support.

My own sixth-grade teachers, Mrs. Gwartzman z"l and Mr. Eisner, in whose classroom I first saw myself as someone who was both creative and could have academic success. Mr. Waldman z"l, for being a loose inspiration for Mr. Sandler.

Dr. Andrea Greenman, for many things but especially for being the first person to say to me, in a way I could hear: "You're a writer."

Cécé Sutton, Pavlina Vyhnalkova, Anna Vhynalkova, and especially Irina Toala, for supporting my family throughout this journey.

My parents, Marilyn and Mendy Maierovitz: Thank you for raising us in a house full of books and Judaism, for supporting my education, and holding your breath along with me for my dreams.

My siblings, Eli Maierovitz, Dov Maierovitz and Shoshana Israel, and Yona and Meir Chaim Dan—you are all the pieces of my locket.

Miriam and Yale Drazin, for being a prototype for the best in-laws anyone could wish for.

My sister- and brother-in-law Meira and Barry Lebovits, for giving me lots of firsthand experience of being in the home of a large, loving, and community-involved family.

And to all the families whose homes I used to love spending time in growing up, as well as to my parents for making our home that place for my friends. And to my children's friends for choosing to spend time in ours.

The text of this book was set in 12 point Warnock Pro, a typeface commissioned by Chris Warnock in honor of his father in 1997, and designed by Robert Slimbach. ✳ The title type was set in KG Bless Your Heart, a font designed by Kimberly Geswein. ✳ The author name was set in Chauncy Decaf Bold, a font designed by Chank Diesel. ✳ The jacket art was created by Shamar Knight-Justice. ✳ The book was printed and bound at LSC Communications. ✳ Production was overseen by Melissa Schirmer. ✳ Manufacturing was supervised by Katie Wurtzel. ✳ The book was designed by Marijka Kostiw and edited by Benjamin Gartenberg and Tracy Mack.